ON THE RESERVATION

He looked out over the quiet, green rolling hills of Benewah and wondered of his future. What was there here, he wondered. What work to earn his living by? What work that was with dignity?

Billy White Hawk often thought of Waluwetsu, the blind one, that spring and summer of his fourteenth year.

Waluwetsu was very old, more than one hundred, he said, and he knew much. Waluwetsu sometimes would say disturbing things, things Billy did not understand that lingered long in the child's mind and troubled him.

"There is little left of what once was," old Waluwetsu would often say, and he would tell Billy of the Manitous, the spirits of earth and wind and sky and rain.

Billy thought how still, some things must have been the same, the sky, the acres of small, rolling hills, the high forested hills, the dark mountains rising in the north, the twisting river. These things which he called Manitous, the wind and rain and sun must have been the way they are now. These must always have been, even when Waluwetsu was a boy and no Suyappi soldier, no black-robed missionary had come.

THE
OWL'S SONG

JANET CAMPBELL HALE

AVON
PUBLISHERS OF BARD, CAMELOT, DISCUS, EQUINOX AND FLARE BOOKS

AVON BOOKS
A division of
The Hearst Corporation
959 Eighth Avenue
New York, New York 10019

ISBN: 0-380-00605-7

First Avon Printing, May 1976

AVON TRADEMARK REG. U.S. PAT. OFF. AND
FOREIGN COUNTRIES, REGISTERED TRADEMARK—
MARCA REGISTRADA, HECHO EN CHICAGO, U.S.A.

Printed in the U.S.A.

THE
OWL'S SONG

PROLOGUE

He was six years old, then. His ma was gone away to the sanitarium. She'd been gone since the spring before. She had the coughing sickness and was very sick for a while but was supposed to be getting better all the time. Billy's dad went to see her every month, leaving Billy at his uncle's, and Dad said she might be coming home by summer. Then she got worse again, suddenly, and Dad went away to be with her. He'd been gone several days.

In winter his dreams were often of warm days, clear skies, sunshine and the earth alive with new green growing things. He lay sleeping and dreaming of these things while outside the harsh winds swept over the snow-covered hills.

In his dream Billy was standing on a high hill when he suddenly turned into a birdlike creature, a boy with beautiful wings growing out from his shoulder blades. He spread his wings and slowly rose a few feet up off the ground. He went higher up into the sky, marveling, feeling the air pass through his feathers. He soared, turning around in the air, flying in widening circles. Higher and higher he went until the earth was far away.

He was drifting in a place where the sky around him was amber and gold and warm.

He saw that the sun was a great glowing sphere of light not far away. Slowly he was coming nearer the sun, closer and closer. He could feel himself beginning to glow and become golden and warm and give off light.

He was very near the sun, about to enter inside when there was suddenly a strange sound and Billy's flight became slower until he was stopped, suspended in the warm air just outside the sun.

The sound was gentle, not loud, at first, as if it were coming from a long way away. It was like the singing of old men with deep, rough voices. The sound became louder and the sun began to lose its light and its warmth and Billy was drawn away from it.

Then, with that strange, chantlike, even sound becoming ever stronger, Billy was himself again, just an ordinary little boy—no longer a bird with wings.

Without his wings he could not fly, could not stop himself from falling. He plunged, faster and faster he fell back down. The hills below seemed to be rushing up at him. At last he hit the surface of the earth and there sank deep, deep inside, slowing in the thick darkness.

He emerged, finally, into wakefulness to find that strange sound still there, deep and strong and real.

He was lying on a pallet on the floor alongside Tom. Tom was his cousin, his uncle's boy, and Tom was nearly five years older than Billy. They were covered with a heavy quilt. The fire was burning very low, the light from the flames shone flickering and dim through the cracks in the stove.

"Tom," he whispered, "hey, Tom." His cousin was lying on his side with his back turned to Billy. He was lying very quiet and still, so quiet Billy couldn't hear him breathing. Billy reached over and touched his shoulder lightly, "You awake?" he whispered.

"Yeah," Tom answered, sighing, "I'm awake," and he turned around toward Billy.

"Tom, what's that? Do you hear it?"

"It's nothing, Silly Billy. Nothing. Just a poor old hooty owl can't find his way home. Go back to sleep, now, Billy."

Billy lay awake though, until the owl went away just before daybreak.

A man came from town the next day. He said Billy's dad called him up. He said Billy's dad would be gone another few days, that his ma had died in the night and he was planning on burying her in the town where the sanitarium was. Billy would always remember that night.

CHAPTER I

It was the springtime of the year Billy White Hawk was fourteen years old. All the ice and snow were gone away, the river's waters ran swift and clear, and the days were warm and filled with sunshine.

Billy was free now that he'd graduated from the eighth grade, free at last of the town school. Never again would he have to go there and sit behind a desk he knew was not meant for him and passively listen to them speak of strange Suyappi things that were without meaning for him. He'd never have to see them looking at him that way with their bright and shallow Suyappi eyes, *through* him, as if he were not there.

It seemed as though this time should be a good one; that Billy should feel more peaceful with the trouble of the school gotten rid of.

Yet now he thought of next fall and then the long winter when he wouldn't be in school and he wondered how it would be then, just Joe and himself to while the hours away, Joe with his drinking and his detective magazines and his cleaning and hauling business. And he thought of the year after that and all the years of his life that would follow. Sometime his father would die. Joe was old already, past sixty-five, and when he died there'd be just Billy.

He looked out over the quiet, rolling hills of Benewah and wondered of his future. What was there here, he wondered. What work to earn his living by? What work that was with dignity?

The Benewah hills lay vast, rolling, empty all around him. The people were so few, so far scattered and, it seemed, always becoming fewer. It was only the old ones now who remained in the Benewah to live out their lives. The young ones always left someday, returning every now and then but never for long.

Billy White Hawk often thought of Waluwetsu, the blind one, that spring and summer of his fourteenth year.

Waluwetsu was very old, more than one hundred, he said, and he knew much. Waluwetsu sometimes would say disturbing things, things Billy did not understand that lingered long in the child's mind and troubled him.

When Billy was very young Waluwetsu told him of the changes; how the world had become so different since he was a boy. He told how once the whole of the Benewah was the people's to live in roaming freely, not confined to one small corner the way it was now. Once there was only the people of the tribe in this country. There was no Suyappi soldier then, no Jesuit missionary, and the land had been wild and free, without roads and houses of any kind, places where trees were chopped down, no torn, plowed, and cultivated fields.

Billy was six or seven then ... he'd tried to think of what Waluwetsu told him. Nothing had changed since he could remember. He could not imagine anything being much different. It was hard to think of there ever being another time before this one; or there ever being one after.

"There is little left of what once was," old

12

Waluwetsu would often say, and he would tell Billy of the Manitous, the spirits of earth and wind and sky and rain.

Billy thought how still, some things must have been the same, the sky, the acres of small, rolling hills, the high forested hills, the dark mountains rising in the north, and twisting river. These things which he called Manitous, the wind and rain and sun must have been the way they are now. These must always have been, even when Waluwetsu was a boy and no Suyappi soldier, no black-robed missionary had come.

"There is little left of what once was," he would say again, and his voice was very sad and Billy would try hard to think of what he was saying, of what his words meant. Still, he could not understand, not then as a small child. It was not until this year when Billy wondered of his future and began to see the world in a different way.

Some things, he'd thought, would never change. And yet, it would end, Waluwetsu said, the people, the reservation, and this way of life.

"There is little left of what once was. The time is coming when even this will be gone—taken away. And we will be no more. The time is coming when the owl's song will be for our race."

CHAPTER II

It was a cloudy, hot afternoon, the air still and heavy and there was the smell of coming rain.

Billy had done his and his father's wash that day—heating the water in tubs on the kitchen stove, keeping a good fire blazing so that it was stifling hot in the small cabin. He was standing in the doorway looking up at the dark sky. A few minutes before he'd heard the first thunder and seen the first lightning. The wash was draped over bushes of wild currants growing near the house alongside what had once been a fence when the old house was there, for pigs, maybe, but was now just a few poles in the ground with small boards connecting them. He stepped off the porch and went to gather the wash and bring it in before the rain started. The dirt was like dust, dry and powderlike under his bare feet. It was about time for a rain, he thought, about time.

Most of the things were dry; all except for the heavy things, like Joe's many-pocketed work pants and the denim overalls. What was dry Billy put in a cardboard carton, not bothering to fold the things or smooth them out. He never did. The wet things he draped over chairs to dry.

Outside it began to rain, softly at first, gently. The raindrops fell onto the dry, loose earth near the door, making little dots of dark mud where they fell, causing the dust in between where the drops fell to rise off the ground from the impact. Soon, though, it was more than dark, wet dots upon the ground; the ground was covered with rain, wet, no longer loose.

The rain hit against the window panes and upon the roof and came in through the open door onto the worn linoleum. Billy was sitting in a big easy chair watching the rain. He liked the way it smelled, the way it made the earth smell when the rain came like this after a long time of being hot and dry. He left the door open and the rain water

14

gathered in a small pool on the floor just inside the doorway.

It was late, almost pitch dark because of the heavy rain clouds but, even so, it would be becoming night now and Joe was still not home.

Billy was tired from the work he'd done, rubbing the soiled clothes on a washboard so that the skin on his knuckles was sore and red, packing all that water from the well, to wash and wash and rinse two times. Billy sat in the chair in the dark watching the rain, smelling the freshness from outside coming in, listening to it hitting, harder now, against the windows and the roof. He didn't light a lamp. He worried about his father. He'd be drinking, of course. He'd stay a long time and become very drunk and then he'd drive that old pickup home over the narrow, sometimes winding roads, slippery in the rain, maneuvering that old truck swiftly along, guiding it while watching with that one eye. Billy watched down the road toward the east. Before the road went around the bend there was only the small, rolling hills in that direction and you could see about two miles. He saw some headlights but these headlights were too big, too bright to be those of the pickup and they traveled along too surely and steadily. Billy watched those headlights anyway, watched them pass by their road without slowing down, watched when the headlights could no longer be seen and there were the two rows of large red taillights, only barely visible, going on toward the west and disappearing there. There was one other set of lights, a car's, before Billy fell asleep. There was always very little traffic on that roadway.

It was very late, almost dawn, when Billy woke up again and it was still raining, harder even than before, spilling from the sky in great torrents. His

15

father had come home. He'd parked the pickup on the other side of the river a way from the house as he often would when there were rain storms. He wanted it to be there should the river overflow its banks and wash away the sturdy log bridge. They could cross on the narrow footbridge that was built higher above the river than the other. Joe said there was a bad flood like that once a long time ago when he was a boy. Billy was not awakened, then, by the rattling noisy truck as he would have been if Joe had driven it up close to the house. It was Joe's footsteps on the porch outside that roused him from sleep. Billy went to help him. He was in bad shape, all right, about as bad as Billy'd ever seen but he was home safe, at least. He'd made it again. Billy took hold of him around the waist and placed his father's arm up over his shoulders and his father leaned his heavy weight against him.

Joe's lip was swollen and cut and he'd been bleeding. He was wearing denim bib overalls, the kind with the heavy metal fasteners and Billy thought the fasteners must have been too hard for him to undo after he got so drunk because he'd peed all over himself and the overalls were smeared with mud on the knees and there was mud on the palms of his hands where he'd fallen in the rain.

The floor was wet and slick because Billy had neglected to shut the door and Joe was leaning heavily upon Billy's shoulders. He was mumbling things Billy couldn't understand and his breath smelled stalely of beer. He was trying now to stand alone and having trouble with his balance.

"Let go. Let go," he was saying, "let go, I say. I can walk by myself. I'm no old man. Let go." And he tried to take Billy's hand away from him.

"That's okay, Dad," Billy told him, "We're almost to your bed." Joe stopped and would go no further with Billy's help. "I can walk by myself," he said, indignant through the drunkenness. Billy let go of him and Joe straightened his back and held his head up. He took a few steps, slowly, carefully, having trouble. He reeled and fell down, cursing as he hit the floor. He lay there a minute or two, flat on his stomach on the floor, his face turned to one side. Billy waited until he was sure Joe was not going to try to get up himself before he went to him to help.

Billy helped him into his room. "My hat. Wait. Wait. My hat," Joe said. "I left my hat at the Big Bear, I have to go back and get it."

"No, Dad, not now. It's too late now. Come on, Dad, time for bed."

Joe tried to turn and go but it was easy for Billy to push him down onto his bed. He promised he would go with him in the morning and they'd find the hat and Joe settled down while Billy worked untying his shoe laces, loosening them and removing the shoes. Joe lay still while Billy finished undressing him. He was lying on the covers and Billy couldn't disturb him so he brought one of the blankets in from his own bed. He thought his father was sleeping but when he covered him he whispered, "Thank you, Billy. You're a good boy."

Billy was in bed, lying in the darkness that was beginning to turn into gray light, listening to the rain hitting the roof overhead, almost sleeping when Joe began to sing.

His song. His manhood song, the one he'd gotten with his vision from the Manitous. He sang loudly, drunkenly. A manhood song gives a man strength and helps protect him.

Billy remembered Joe had told him once how

17

he'd sung that song when he was a soldier. He was a young warrior then, fighting the Germans over in France. He told Billy how there'd been bullets passing by in the air so near he could feel the wind they made and no bullet would touch him as long as he sang that song, yet other men were falling down dead on the ground all around him.

Billy went to sleep again listening to his father singing his manhood song.

CHAPTER III

The long days of summer passed slowly and one was much like all the others. Joe was gone most of the time, some days doing hauling and cleaning in the town, some days he'd spend from noon on at the Big Bear Saloon. Some nights Joe would be gone drinking until late. Nights at home were quiet, solitary ones, reading his detective magazines by the flame of the kerosene lamp. Always, it seemed, Billy was alone. And always more troubled.

Billy's sleep was filled with awful dreams which came back again and again. In one he was lost in a dense forest. He would be struggling, fighting his way through, trying to find a way out but he was only becoming more lost; the woods, becoming darker and more tangled. Still, he'd push on, climbing over and crawling under the twisting, tangled branches until finally he was caught fast and unable to move. In another dream he'd be lost in the same forest but find his way out. Then he'd see that where the woods ended so did the world itself end, and he would fall off the edge into timeless, empty, black space.

Billy took long walks trying to think of things. He noticed how the days were becoming cooler and knew it would be an early winter that year. He wondered if the days of his life would all be the same as this summer's days had been.

He thought of Tom, his cousin, who'd been gone from the Benewah going on two years, a fighting man now in Viet Nam's jungles. He remembered the good times they'd had growing up, the way Tom always laughed and made fun of him when he was foolishly afraid, laughed until Billy had to laugh too, making his fear go away. He remembered how Tom had explained confusing things—the way it was with girls, with men and women together. Tom had taught him how to hunt, to track and shoot, how to hold his beer, and to use his fists. He thought of these things and he wished for Tom to be with him. Tom would tell him how it was, Tom, who'd been out in the world now and knew how it was. (What a super-warrier, he thought, Tom must make. Brave and strong as he is, and full of spirit, probably killed a lot of enemy soldiers and did lots of brave deeds.) Tom would make him see his worries better, that they were of no big importance, just like when they were growing up.

He thought of his mother, too, those long summer days. He wondered what might've been if his mother had not died and he tried to picture her but the picture was vague and all he could recall was that she'd had small, soft hands, and that she was soft and warm to touch and the smell of her was clean.

He remembered Waluwetsu, maybe most of all. He thought of all the things Waluwetsu had told him ... the things about a boy and how he became a man. A boy had to go looking for his manhood vision. He had to make his heart and body pure, so that the Manitous would see and decide him worthy. Manitous would send a vision and a song, they'd tell him what his man's name was. The strength given him would help him when his body needed it, and it would help when his spirit was weak and sick. Billy thought more and more of the manhood vision and the Manitous and he began watching his dreams very carefully for some sign that would tell him what to look for.

Sometimes in the evenings, in the twilight between day and night, he would go down beside the river and he would lie there in the long, wild grass and with all his being he would will the Manitous to send a vision.

He would lie very still and quiet and listen to the waters of the river passing and look up into the clear sky and try to make it so that his heart and soul were open to such things as visions, so that if there were Manitous watching nearby they'd know he needed help. He would lie in the grass until twilight had passed into night, then get up and walk slowly home again.

For the first three weeks of August Billy watched for a sign from the Manitous and went each evening down by the river to wait. The trees that grew near the river's edge lost their greenness and became shades of yellow and brown and red. The green hills became yellow and all through the Benewah, though the days remained warm, there was the smell, the feel of winter in the air. There was no sign from the Manitous, no dream, no sound ... nothing. Waluwetsu, he thought, that old man who remembered so well what once was, and would not let go. People said that old man was crazy his last few years, that he first would not recognize the voices of those who came to visit and got confused. Later, he would not hear their voices at all and only spoke in the Salishan tongue to people he knew in his youth—people dead for many years. Billy felt the coming winter, the coming years he knew nothing of and he felt foolish that he'd been looking for Manitous, that he'd taken Waluwetsu's words seriously.

It was almost September when Tom came home again, gaunt and tired looking, deeply tanned. He was a corporal now and he had won a medal. "They kicked me out, Billy. I was too much for them." He laughed. Let out early, he said, for some reason he didn't understand, quite. Billy was glad to see Tom and Tom was glad to see Billy. It had been a long time and they had a lot to talk about.

Tom had been back three days and Billy had told him the local news, who'd gotten married, had babies, died, got drafted. And Tom had told Billy stories of Viet Nam, the pretty girls there and their ways, of the funny things that had happened during his army days, and the big cities and lush jungles he'd seen.

Now Billy wanted to talk to Tom of the way he'd been feeling lately, to tell him of his doubts and worries of not knowing what lay ahead and wishing he did. Tom had seen the world outside the Benewah hills, a lot of the world.

They had said everything it seemed and were sitting together quietly when Billy asked him.

"Tom, what are you going to do now?" And the older young man looked at him questioningly. "I mean ... I mean now that you're all done with army life, Tom ... now what?"

Tom smiled a smile that was neither happy nor amused. He looked down at his hands ... "Oh, well, Billy, I don't rightly know. I never did make any plans. Just sort of figured I'd wait and see, take things as they come."

Billy said nothing. He waited for Tom to go on, to say more than that. He had to say more than that. In another minute he did, still looking down at his big hands lying in his lap. "You know, Billy, I was fighting a war just now. Made a few tight buddies, saw some of them get killed. I got so's I sort of quit thinking like in terms of what's going to happen tomorrow or the next day or when I get out. Hanging on, keeping alive, watching out every minute, every second. Living that way you don't think of plans."

He'd not talked much of the war and it was something else Billy'd wanted to hear about. The fighting and the brave warrior's deeds.

"What was it like, Tom? Not the country. The war, the fighting. What was that like, Tom? How many of those enemy soldiers did you kill? A lot, I bet."

And Tom, sitting in the big chair, sat way back and seemed to sink into it and become small. He was looking straight ahead at the wall just a few feet away but seemed to be looking a long, long way away.

"I killed a few, I guess, like most everyone. I guess I did kill a few, all right. Funny thing, you know, Bill ... before the actual fighting and killing I couldn't wait to start right in. I wanted action. Then ..."

"How was it, Tom?" Billy asked. He was listening carefully, wanting Tom to go on with the telling.

"It was just awful at first, Billy. It tears your guts out. At night when you sleep you wake up with bad dreams, sometimes screaming, sometimes having to vomit. Sometimes you just lay there feeling awful and remembering and wishing you never came there and saw such things. And even though you don't really much believe in God you pray to Him and say, 'Dear God, just get me out of this. Let things go back to the way they were before and I'll never ask another thing.'

"Then after a while you get used to it, to the killing. And then it's even worse in a way. Makes you feel kind of like your brain and heart must be burned out, you know, like what's happening is not *really* happening; that guy isn't really you and the whole thing loses its . . . its,"—he lifted his hands as if trying to find the word he wanted—"horror. It's bad to feel that way, you know, not to be able to feel anything about shooting somebody, to just cut off a man's life. Very bad." And then quietly, as an afterthought, "There's no glory in it, Billy. If anybody says any different, don't you believe them." And Tom sighed and slowly raised his long, lean body up from the chair. He stood and stretched, yawned elaborately. He walked over to the open door and looked out at the dull, yellow hills. It was a cool, sunny day outside, a little windy. He stepped out onto the porch and Billy followed. They sat together on the porch watching the empty hills. A small whirlwind passed by, carrying away small rocks and loose, dry surface dirt.

"How's about going fishing, Bill?" Tom asked.

"There's none just now, Tom," he answered, "at least none will bite."

23

In late summer the water of the river was too low to swim in. They didn't feel much like talking any more. They were all talked out and feeling bored and restless now. Billy got up and went back inside. He picked up one of his comic books, one of those adventure things with mutant-like heroes and he began to read the words one by one, his mind not paying attention to what the words were saying. Tom came in and stood beside the davenport where Billy lay reading.

"Hey, Billy," he said loudly, "I got an idea. Why don't we go pick up Mary Lou and get some beer. We could go over to my folks' place, since your dad's going to be back after a while. Nobody home over there until sometime late tonight."

Mary Lou Vargas was a Mexican girl Tom had run around with a little before we went away. She lived in Baker, the little city some sixty or seventy miles away. She was only a little older than Billy, just a young girl, but she wore tight clothes and lots of black goo around her eyes. She was good to Tom, gave him what he wanted from her and wasn't always bugging him and he liked her, though he had another girl, one he talked of marrying in Oregon somewhere. Billy didn't want to go along though. He thought it would be better if Tom and Mary Lou went over to Tom's folks' place alone. He thought the two of them could do without *him* tagging along.

"I can't go, Tom," Billy said, "I can't just walk out and leave this here comic book." But Tom coaxed, "Aw, c'mon, Bill. Maybe she has a friend," he said, "come on along, hell!" And he wanted to go. Anything would be better, Billy thought, than hanging around the house reading comics and waiting for the day to be over.

Tom had his dad's car, an old Chevy, and he

said Billy could drive until they started to get near the town and the traffic became heavier. Billy liked driving. Joe said he was too young to learn to drive the old pickup. "Maybe next year," he'd told him, "when you can get your license." It felt good to get behind the wheel and go cruising on down the road. It had a feel to it of power and freedom. Once or twice Tom had to warn him, "Hey, take it easy, Bill. Slow down a little." Billy was enjoying driving so much he would have liked to spend the whole day like that, up and down the back roads, just driving the car.

When they got to Mary Lou's place, a dumpy little house with yellow brick siding on the edge of town, she came running out to meet them before Tom had even turned off the engine. There was a lot of hugging and kissing between Mary Lou and Tom. He liked his uniform, she said. It made him look older, *like a real man,* she giggled. Her sister, Yolanda, was there too, and she agreed to come along with them.

Billy and Tom had to wait a long time while the girls put on their make-up and changed their clothes and did those things, Billy thought, girls always think they have to do if someone is waiting.

Tom bought a couple of cases of beer before they left town. The man didn't even ask to see his I.D. and that was lucky. It must have been the uniform, Mary Lou giggled, and the rest agreed and they all laughed.

It was a nice, sunny summer day. Tom was home again. There was cause for Billy to feel good. And Billy thought Yolanda was a pretty girl. She was not really much like her sister, though, he thought, she tried to be, the way she dressed and fixed herself up and all. But she was nice. Not loud and laughing all the time. She was just a nice girl,

25

kind of shy, quiet, and easy to talk to. She had big brown eyes and long lashes that curled. She was very small and thin, and just Billy's own age. She could have been younger, even. He liked her and he was glad he'd come along.

Tom's folks' place was just a few miles over the hills from Billy's. It was a small, old place. They were even worse off than Billy and Joe. Tom's dad didn't work much and he didn't have the army disability check coming in either, like Joe did, and he drank a lot. The place was uncared for. It was unpainted and weathered gray-brown and the nails were red with rust. It had no foundation, even, but stood propped up on cement blocks. There was an old woodshed near the house that was almost falling down and many boards were missing.

When they got there Tom and Billy carried the beer inside the house. The house had only two rooms, a bedroom with a double bed where the folks slept and a kitchen with a canvas cot against one wall where Tom's sister slept. Tom was anxious to get Mary Lou in the big bed. Billy told him to go ahead first. He would rather be alone with his girl when he did it, he told Tom, and besides, he was not so anxious as Tom was. Billy didn't feel much like doing it right then, he said.

The truth was, Billy didn't know *how* to do it. He had never in his life done it with a girl; but he was ashamed to have Tom know this. Billy told him to go ahead first. "I'll get mine later," he said, and they laughed together. Tom winked at him and Billy felt a little dumb. He was fourteen years old, almost fifteen. Tom was only twelve, he once told Billy, *his* first time. It was decided, then, that Yolanda and Billy would wait. Billy took a few beers with him and went on outside.

It was very pleasant waiting with Yolanda. They

26

took an old brown army blanket from the car and spread it out in the shade of the woodshed. There were no trees anywhere nearby ... the forested high hills were fives miles in the south and the river was way over near Billy's place at its closest point.

They had a beer, and then another one and they talked. They were shy with one another at first; not even looking into each other's eyes when they talked. Soon, though, the shyness began to melt a little and they were easier being together.

Billy told her about his first hunt the winter before last, how Tom and he had gone together and Billy shot his first deer and he described it to her, "Beautiful, near as tall as me ... a big, fast buck with antlers this wide." On her part, Yolanda told of the town in Texas her family had moved from because her father could get a job in Baker. She told him how she missed that little Texas town and her friends and relatives there, and would go back one day when she was old enough.

Mostly, though, Yolanda just listened and asked questions and smiled and laughed at the appropriate moments.

The sunlight moved around to the side of the shed where Billy and Yolanda were and Tom and Mary Lou were still in the house. Billy opened up two more bottles of beer. It was nice. It felt so good, just lying there in the sun with a pretty girl, talking, and drinking the cool beer.

He looked at her and she smiled at him and then without even thinking about it he leaned over and kissed her ... a short, gentle, light kiss and it was nice. Her mouth was so soft and warm, he thought, and he marveled that a girl's mouth could be that way. Her lipstick tasted sweet. He held her and kissed her again and she returned his kiss and

27

pulled him close against her hard little breasts, winding her arms around his neck when his kiss became deeper. Billy was surprised and deeply pleased. He thought, maybe later, after Tom and Mary Lou are finished in there ... then maybe we can go inside, Yolanda and me. He held the girl close to him and he was so excited he was almost trembling. Maybe today I'll do it too, he thought. He closed his eyes tightly against the summer afternoon sun.

Then Billy heard Tom yelling and Mary Lou shrieking. "My God," she screamed. "Fire Fire!" A fire had started in the house. Billy and Yolanda let go of each other and rose to their feet. Tom and Mary Lou came bounding out of the house, pulling their clothes on. "My shoes," Mary Lou wailed, "I left my shoes in there."

Billy could see the flames now, and feel the heat of the blaze. It was a big fire already, too big to try to control. The flames rose higher and the fire crackled. There was nothing anyone could do but watch. They heard the loud popping sound as the bottles of beer inside the house became hot and exploded. The house was small. The fire burned quickly. It didn't take long for it to burn down. In a few minutes all that was left were the cement blocks the house had been standing upon and the black, smoking remains of the boards. They were still standing there, all four of them, Mary Lou barefoot and her blouse buttoned crookedly, when Clara came.

Clara was Tom's sister, and she was a year older than he was. She came riding the old spotted horse over the hills. She rode the horse very fast and it was sweating and breathing hard by the time she reached them. She jumped down from the horse and looked at Tom, and then at Billy, from one to the other. Her face was not shocked, not surprised or stunned, but angry. Very, very angry.

She could not speak through her anger at first. She made an attempt but could not say anything. She waited a minute and then began again. She yelled at Tom. She stood in front of him yelling and carrying on, still holding the spotted horse's reins in one hand. She was just a small woman, more than a head shorter than Tom. She had to look up at him.

"You dirty, no good, drunken bum!" Her voice was tight.

"It was an accident," he said meekly. He looked down at the ground, away from her eyes ... "A ... cigarette."

"You bastard!" his sister screamed. "You never think of anything, do you? You just go on about your own careless, selfish, stupid way and you don't consider anybody!" Her face was red now, flaming red, her eyes round and wild-looking. She began to cry. Her voice cracked and it was hard for her to go on.

"All you have ever caused us is trouble with your fighting and stealing and drunken ways. Trouble. Shame. All you have ever been. Oh, my God. Look at what you've done now." And she gestured with one hand toward the smoking black ruins where the house had been. "That was all we had and you had to come and take it away from us. Oh, what will we do." Now Clara turned on Billy:

"You. You stupid, blind little puppy, always following this useless troublemaker around. Look at him. Look at your great hero. What is he good for? I hope you watched carefully. I hope you learned your lesson well." The last sentence she pronounced weakly, her voice becoming thin and without power. Her rage had been spent. She

29

dropped the reins and hid her face in her hands, weeping noisily, her small shoulders heaving. Tom tried to comfort her, to take her in his arms but she pulled away from him.

"Go away!" she shouted. "Go away! Both of you just get out of here. I don't want to look at you. Why did you have to come back here, Tom, why? Why?" There seemed nothing he could do, nothing he could say, nor for Billy either.

They climbed in the car, Tom and Billy in the front seat, the two girls together in back. Tom started the motor and pulled away from there. Billy looked back once to where the house had been. Clara was sitting on the ground before the smoldering, burned place, the spotted horse standing still beside her. She held her face in her hands and was crying.

Tom did not say anything while he drove. The girls in the back seat looked frightened. Once Mary Lou asked him to take them home but he seemed not to hear her and didn't answer. He just kept on driving, his dark eyes aimed straight ahead, his jaw tight. Billy didn't ask him where he was going or what he was going to do. He thought maybe he just felt overwhelmed because of the damage he'd caused and he needed to drive fast like that for a while. It might make him feel a little better. Billy didn't feel good, either. He leaned back and shut his eyes and let the cool breeze coming in the window wash over his face.

Tom drove several hours before he finally stopped the car. They were off the reservation by then, up in the mountains where it was cool and tall trees grew all around and it was green all over. Tom had driven up a narrow dirt road. He sat there a minute or two with the motor turned off. It was very quiet and still up there, the air noticeably thinner. Billy sat quietly, wondering what Tom was going to do. He listened to the sound of his own even, steady breathing.

"Billy," Tom said at last, still with his dark eyes staring straight ahead, "you know, Clara was right. One hundred per cent! I *am* a good-for-nothing. All my life it's been bad. Never caused my family, nor anybody else either, nothing but bad times and troubles, just like she said back there a while ago. Trying to look ahead, Bill, well I can't see anything there either. I think the time is here for me ... for me"—his voice was tight, strained, seemed to have snagged—"to go away now, to leave for good and stop causing bad things."

He opened the door and got out. He walked back behind the car. Billy heard him unlocking and opening the trunk, then slamming it closed again. Then he walked over to Billy's side and Billy saw that he was holding the .22 in his hands. He motioned with his head for Billy to come with him. He opened his door, shut it behind him, and followed as Tom turned and began walking away. The girls were talking excitedly, shrilly to one another in Spanish.

They walked only a little way away from the road, up over a small hill just out of view of the car. Billy didn't know what to say ... what he *could* say ... what he could do. He was scared too, more scared than he could ever in his life remember being and he was shaking. He didn't want Tom to do that. He wanted Tom to keep on being alive, he loved the guy more than if he'd been a brother and he didn't want him to die. He knew he had no right to stop Tom, though. And he knew he wouldn't be able to even if he did try.

"We don't have to go no further," Tom said, stopping. He looked around as if watching for someone or something. "This is as good a place as any. I want to write a note to my girl, Clemma. You must mail it to her for me. Let her know my last thoughts were of her. Promise me, Billy." Billy nodded. His throat was dry, painfully dry. He watched as Tom tore open a cigarette package and used the white paper inside to write his note on. He folded it and handed it to Billy. Billy reached out and took it and put it in the front pocket of his shirt. Tom laid his hand heavily on his shoulder. "You won't forget, now, Billy?"

"No, I won't forget," Billy said quietly. Tom began to cry a little then, turning his face away from Billy. Billy had never seen Tom, nor any other man, cry before. He felt scared and sick.

Tom wiped the tears from his eyes and lifted the .22. His arms were very long for he was a tall man. Billy could see he would be able to do it. He was able to reach the trigger while holding it to his head, though just barely. Billy moved his eyes away from him, not wanting to see, wishing he were somewhere, *anywhere* else. He looked up at the sky. It was getting late now. The deep blue had begun to fade and the sun was gone down. It was getting cold. It would soon be dark.

Billy heard the little click. Seconds later the big bang as the .22 went off and echoed loudly. He heard the frightened, piercing screams of the girls in the car down the hill. He would not at first look away from the sky. He took a deep breath and reluctantly turned back again.

When the gun fired, it was with great force and had caused Tom to jump far up from the ground and when he fell again it was past the top of the small hill and he'd begun to roll down, toward the car. He fell first backward, his feet going up in the air, over his head and back again, then he rolled more smoothly. He stained the grass red with his blood. It was everywhere. Billy walked down the hill, going as slowly as he could. God, he thought, Oh God! Tom, you could have found a better way. Oh God. It was bad. Very, very bad.

Tom was not dead. He hadn't done it. Not quite. He'd rolled so that half of his body was under the car now. He was quivering, shaking. The blood was thick in his black hair and covered his face, was already drying where it no longer flowed. It had soaked his khaki army shirt red.

The two girls were crying and hugging each other, whimpering, hiding their faces. Tom's eyes rolled back so that only the white parts showed.

Billy was standing over him, watching horrified as he realized that Tom was alive. His lips were moving but he could make no sound. Billy walked up close, bent over his cousin. He heard him whisper something but couldn't make out what it was. He said it again ... a second, a third, a fourth time. "Again," he whispered, "shoot me again," and Billy could not. Tom was lying on the ground wanting, trying to die and Billy couldn't move. He felt a coward. He couldn't help him in his suffering. He couldn't shoot him. Then while Billy watched, Tom suddenly stopped quivering and lay still. Billy waited ... ten seconds, twenty, thirty, a full minute. He reached down and took Tom's wrist, lifted it and felt for the pulse. He was dead.

Billy had to pull the body out from under the car. Tom was heavy. And then he had to search through the pockets of Tom's pants to find the keys to the ignition.

It was just dark by the time he headed the car back down again toward home.

Billy took the girls home first. It was late when he finally got back to the place. Joe was there and

33

he was sober. He'd fallen asleep while reading and the lamp still burned and Joe still held an open detective magazine. Billy woke him and told his dad what had happened. He would leave it up to Joe to go tell the police, or the coroner, or whoever and take care of whatever else had to be done.

Billy went out on the porch and sat and rested and was alone. He tried not to think of anything. It would only be a little while before the police came and he would have to tell it all the way it happened ... to make himself remember it all again in detail. He wished there was some way he could make it be just twelve hours earlier.

Joe came out the door and walked past him and down the steps. Billy watched him as he walked over to the Chevy and got in and drove away. Billy felt bad. He was tired. So tired.

He sat on the porch a long time, alone in the dark, before he heard the old Chevy that belonged to Tom's folks. He didn't know at first whether it was Tom's folks coming or his own dad returning.

It was Tom's dad, as it turned out, his uncle, Nicademus. He watched Nicademus climb out. He slammed the car door shut and walked toward the house. He'd come alone. Billy wondered what he could want. What had he come here for?

Nicademus walked up the steps and stood in front of Billy, one foot on the porch, the other still on the last step. He pushed his hat up away from his face, took his cigarettes from the pocket of his shirt, and a book of matches. He lit one up. Billy saw his face a moment in the light from the match. He put the match out and threw it away in the dust. He inhaled deeply. He leaned an elbow on the thigh of the leg that was raised. Billy could barely see him in the pale moonlight. He could see his profile, black against the dark blue night sky

... the big, bent nose, the strong chin. He thought how Nicademus looked a lot like Tom had looked. Nicademus cleared his throat

"Billy," he began, his voice strong in the darkness, smooth and deep, "your dad came over where we're staying a while ago. Told us what happened." Billy waited for him to go on, to say whatever it was he'd come there to say.

"Now, you know, Billy, Tom's mother and I, well, we're sorry this happened. We wish it didn't. Tom was wrong to do this. He was our boy. We wish he was still alive."

Billy's uncle paused, taking another deep drag from his cigarette, and exhaling it slowly. He went on: "But, you know, there's another way of looking at this. We lost everything in the fire. We have nothing left. No money. Nothing. Try to understand, son, the way it is. Try to understand what I'm going to ask you to do." Billy nodded in the darkness though he knew his uncle was not looking at him.

"You see, Tom left some insurance money. We need it badly. No one must know it was a suicide. They have to think it was an accident. Do you understand, Bill? We have nothing. We lost all we had."

Billy told him yes, he understood, though he did not. Yes, he said, yes, he would say it was an accident.

Nicademus stood there, his foot propped up on the porch a while longer, until he'd finished his cigarette. Then he threw it down on the ground and walked back to the car. He drove away into the night. It was very quiet when the sound of the Chevy's engine died away.

The police came the next day. Joe was gone into town and Billy was alone at the house. He talked to them sitting outside on the front porch. It didn't take long and it was not so hard as Billy had expected. They'd already talked to the girls.

"Oh, that," Billy said, "We were just fooling around. We were just trying to scare those girls. No, he didn't leave a note. He didn't mean to do it. He was just fooling around. We went up there and he held the gun to his head. We were just trying to scare those girls was all. Then the .22 went off ... accidentally. And he died."

After they left, Billy went inside and found the shirt he was wearing yesterday and reached in the pocket. He took the note Tom had given him to mail to the girl in Oregon. He lit a match to it and watched it burn.

CHAPTER IV

In the late morning most all of the clouds went away and the sun came out. Billy had been sitting alone on the front porch watching empty hills. It was as if he was caught, numb and still, in that instant right after he'd burned Tom's note. I am through with it now, he'd said to himself. I have nothing more to do with it. And then the numbness began. He did not find it unpleasant.

Then Joe came home and told him, "In three day's time, Billy—early the morning of the third day," and Billy nodded. He knew his father meant the burial. His father would be going to the wake soon, no doubt; he would be interested. He would stay there, wherever it was being held, until the burial the morning of the third day. He would expect Billy to be interested too, to want to come along. He didn't know that Billy was through with it now and wanted no more part of it.

When his father passed him and went inside Billy remained as he was before but now the instant had passed. Still there was a sort of numbness but not as tranquil and all-encompassing as before. He shuddered as if a sudden chill had touched him. He didn't want to be alone.

Billy went and stood in the doorway, leaned against the frame and watched his father shave.

Joe stood in front of the mirror that hung on the wall above the washstand and lathered his face with soap. His beard was not heavy and he disliked shaving. Except on special occasions he would shave only every other Friday. It had been less than a week, Billy remembered.

He went about the task with a straight razor, slowly, carefully. He relathered twice. Billy could remember as a small boy watching his father this way, fascinated, wishing he were grown up enough to shave too. At length Billy's father was finished and his round face was smooth-shaven and shiny, without one cut or nick.

Joe went about his getting ready while Billy watched. I can't go, he shouted to himself, and: I don't want to be left alone. Maybe Joe would know. Maybe he would be able to feel the way it was with Billy and stay with him.

When Joe was all ready, his starched white shirt buttoned to the very last one, and the vest and suit jacket donned he asked Billy, "Are you staying?" "Yes," he said. Billy walked with Joe out to the pickup.

"Dad." Billy said quietly just before his father climbed up into the cab of the truck. Dad. The word itself was all he meant to say. He was not asking a question, not addressing him. Dad was who this person was to him. He'd never seen Joe looking quite so old before as he did then—standing in the harsh sunlight—the deep lines were easy to see, the wrinkles around his eyes, the looseness of the skin on his throat. He was looking at him waiting to hear something from Billy. He was looking at him with that one, dark, shiny eye of his, narrowed to a slit in the glare of the sunlight, the other sightless one open wide, staring crazily upward and in the opposite direction.

"Dad," Billy said, "I'm finished with it, Dad. I want it to be all gone and over with."

"I'll be back, son, before noon in three days." And he opened the door of the pickup and pulled himself up, holding onto the inside handle. Billy watched him leaving. It took quite a while to take that old truck down the bumpy, rutted dirt road but once he reached the pavement he turned it eastward and in a few seconds had sped out of sight.

Billy was lying on his back on the ground, his eyes closed. The light shone through his eyelids warm and reddish. Then a mass of clouds passed between Billy and the sun and there was only blackness. He was lying very still, concentrating on making the muscles of his body relax. *Think of nothing. Be calm.* That was the way to bring sleep to a weary body. Turn off the troubled mind, let it go. The inconstant light was distracting and so was the faint sound of the river passing (like the soft voices of many young women, whispering, sighing, singing. *Ahaha Ahahah* went the river. *Ahahah*, on and on). He was aware of his own breathing, the

38

constant rise and fall, the taking in of new air, the release of the used. And of his heartbeat, so even and strong and sure.

It was not easy, thinking of nothing. There was the picture of Tom he could not seem to rid himself of for long. It would be all right, it seemed, and then just when he thought he had it all under control there it would be again, suddenly, horrible and vivid.

There was Tom all covered with blood and his eyes rolled back and his lips moving, whispering that last plea. Billy was very tired. His body ached. He opened his eyes and got up. He walked down by the river.

He was barefoot and the sharp rocks cut and bruised the soles of his feet but he hardly noticed. He took no care in where he stepped. He felt as though inside himself, in his chest, was a bad thing, a horrible and evil thing growing and pounding to be let out, threatening to break out and take hold of him. He could not allow this thing to reach the surface. He must keep it locked deep in the darkness of himself.

Think of nothing. Think of nothing. Or turn away to other things? He felt the pain in the soles of his feet and he noticed how low the waters of the river ran, how weak and feeble the current. *Look at things. See how usual. The world is not changed. This bad time will be gone.*

He looked up at the sky, at the rich blue color of it and the white-mist clouds floating, drifting, making big, moving shadows over the hills. He looked at the sun through the branches of the birch trees that grew along the river's edge and he saw how few leaves were left, how already many had fallen and lay dry and dead in layers upon the ground. He noticed the difference of the autumn sunlight

39

from the summer's. The sun had begun traveling away from the earth.

He waded out into the middle of the river. The water was as cold as ice. It did not quite reach his waist. He lowered his body into the water, bending at the knees, until only his head was above water. The cold seemed less and not so hard to endure. He moved his hands about in the water, held his breath, and ducked his head under until his lungs ran out of air. He surfaced gasping for breath. His wet hair hung down over his eyes and stuck to his face. He laughed foolishly and pushed his hair back. *It will be all right. It is as before. Nothing has happened.* Then, suddenly, Tom. Tom, again, his lips silently forming those words: Shoot me again. Again. That awful thing expanding and wanting to be let out.

Billy got out of the water and walked, barefoot and soaking wet, up into the high, forested hill that rose behind the house. It was late now. The sun was almost gone and it was getting colder. That thing, whatever it was, would have to go away. He knew part of it was fear and there was no sense in being afraid.

Billy remembered a day a long, long time ago when he was just a little boy, before his mother went away. A raging storm had come up and for some reason Joe was not there, big strong Joe with his way of taking care of things. There was just Billy and his gentle, frail mother at home. Thunder shook the earth, it seemed, lightning tore open the sky—rain fell in great torrents and wind thrust it back up again and whipped it against the sides of the house and against the window glass so hard it looked like it would break. Billy screamed and ran to his mother. He clung to her, trembling with fear and crying. She held him. She put her warm, soft arms around him and he hid his face in her breast.

"Shhhh, don't cry, shhhhh," she told him, stroking his hair. "Don't be afraid, little man. Mamma's here. Mamma will keep you safe." After a time the storm subsided a bit and Billy was comforted. He left his mother's arms and went to play with his wooden blocks again, stacking them, forming houses and walls and towers. When he heard the thunder boom outside, a quick pang of fear shot through him but he kept hold and wouldn't be fearful: Mamma's here. She will keep you safe, he told himself. Soon he went to the window and looked out. He felt afraid again. He wanted to cry out and run into his mother's arms. He did not. He stood watching the storm.

So this is the way it is, he thought, with Manitous and such things. He saw the fury of the storm. His mother was there but it made no difference, good or bad. His mother was, as all people, very small and powerless in comparison to the Manitous. The storm could not be made to leave or be more gentle.

He heard the loud thunder. He saw the bolts of lightning tear open the sky. He tried to make himself calm. Being afraid did no good. He would just have to make courage for himself and wait until the storm ended, and hope that it would be soon.

Other times he'd done this too, made courage for himself when he felt small and powerless. Being afraid never did any good, never helped.

It was the same way now, he felt. He had to try hard not to be afraid. He had to keep moving.

By nightfall Billy was miles from the house.

Exhausted, he lay down on the ground in a place where the trees parted. Clouds had gathered in the sky and hid the moon and stars so there was only darkness and below him Billy could hear the coyotes howling. The coyotes moved to different locations, calling to one another, moving again, farther away. It was cold now and Billy's clothes were still damp.

He curled up into as small a person as he could make of himself against the trunk of a fallen tree. Far away the coyotes still howled. He closed his eyes and rested, only half-sleeping because of the cold.

He thought of his father and his father's search for his manhood vision:

It was a long time ago his father told of the vision. Waluwetsu had told Billy that his father was among the last of those to seek the vision, and Billy'd asked him to tell about it. He was small at the time of the telling. The way Joe told of it, though, made Billy see it all happen very clearly so it was real to him and he'd never forgotten.

"Well, I will tell you, then, Billy. I will tell you as best I can the way it was as it happened, the way I remember it.

"I was about twelve or fourteen, around that age. Anyway, it was that summer I came home from Oklahoma. They took us and made us go to government school. We didn't know English, us boys they took, and we didn't understand what was happening. We rode a train all the way to Oklahoma. Now, we'd not seen the wars ourselves, the way the Suyappi came and killed so many of our people but we heard lots of stories of such things from our parents or grandparents. We were afraid maybe they were taking us somewhere to kill us. Some of the older boys had had a vision of manhood and on the train they sang their songs. Those of us who *hadn't,* listened to them and it made us feel better.

"So it turned out to be a government school. We were put in with Kiowas and Navajos and Comanches, only boys not of our own tribe so that we had to speak English. In two years' time I was allowed to come home. It was a very troubled summer, I remember. I'd learned a lot. I was not sure of many things. That was when I asked my father to tell me how to contact the Manitous and he told me.

"I went up into the hills. I went by myself. For four days and four nights I searched for my vision. I did not eat. I did not sleep. I tried to make my body and spirit pure. I watched the skies and I listened to the wind. I opened my heart. I waited.

"It was on the fourth night of my vigil I saw it. At first it was only a star up in the sky and I noticed how it seemed bigger and brighter than all the others. I fixed my eyes to that star and as I watched, it seemed that the star grew and its light became more. Then I realized the star was moving, and very quickly moving, down from the sky toward the earth. I was afraid. I did not move. It came closer each minute. At last the light hovered in the sky right above where I was sitting. It was huge—a white body of light. It made the hills all around like daytime. Still I watched. It came no closer.

"Soon I felt myself rising up off the ground. Not my body, but my spirit. My spirit separated from my body and went up into the body of white light and became a part of it. I could look down and see my body sitting on the ground as before.

"I cannot explain the way it was. I talked with the Manitous, all right, but it was not like this. It

43

was a much different way of talking, a language not of words. I knew truth, though I cannot translate or explain. I understood perfectly all the truth concerning life and death and spirits and the ways and reasons for being. My name, they said; Sa-húlt-sum, He-Who-Searches.

"Toward the end of night my spirit returned to my body and the white light began to fade. When morning came there was a wind and on the wind I heard my song. With gladness in my heart I began singing that song and I felt good and I felt strong. It was with my man's voice I sang."

Sa-húlt-sum had fallen silent then for many minutes. His eyes were closed. Billy thought of the vision, remembered, saw it all. Then Sa-húlt-sum said, "Anyway that is the way I remember it. It may not have been like that but that is how it seems. Your mother, now, was a good Christian lady, Billy. She said it could not have been."

In the morning Billy came fully awake, cold and damp, his body aching and more tired than when he'd lain down to rest. The sky was lightly overcast. In the north above the mountains he saw black clouds had gathered. He walked back to the house and slept all of that day and all of the following night.

Billy was well rested, then, by the time Joe came home again the third day and his mind was not bothered as before with the memory of Tom's dying. "They buried him alongside his grandfather, Billy, you know the place," Joe said. He thought of Tom lying alongside White Hawk, the shaman. White Hawk, Waluwetsu had said, had powers other men didn't have. He knew the Manitous in a way other men didn't and his medicine made well ailments of body and spirit. White Hawk didn't teach any of his eight sons, as was the way, his

44

shaman's knowledge. White Hawk had been the tribe's last shaman. "He has no headstone yet. It will take a few months. Etta chose a fine one for him. The veterans will pay the cost, you know. One of white marble, small, but a very fine headstone." Joe did not seem troubled. He'd seen so much dying in his lifetime. Joe went into his room and lay down and slept a long time then, though he still wore his white shirt and suit.

When Joe woke up it was late at night. He looked for Billy and found him sitting on the porch.

"It's cold out," Joe said, and Billy answered, "Yeah, it seems the good days are near over now." The coyotes were howling again. By the sound of them it seemed they were in a half circle, a pack of maybe six or seven, a wide half circle in the hills above. First one would howl and then another one closest to him, and the next and on and on until the first began again. Joe came and sat alongside Billy. He'd lit the lamp inside. The dim light shone through the windows and open door.

"No more mosquitoes," Billy said. "Are you hungry, Dad?" Joe shook his head no. "Not hungry, still tired. It feels so strange to sleep during daylight hours and wake up when it's pitch dark like this." Billy nodded. "Uh-huh."

"It mixes you up," Joe said, "I thought it was early morning when I woke up." They sat there awhile.

Then Billy said, "Dad, remember when you told me about when you did that thing, you know, I mean that *vigil* thing like they used to do? I mean when you saw that big white light."

"Yeah, son, I remember telling you. You were just a little kid then. I remember." Billy waited. He wanted his dad to tell him about it all again. He turned his head away from Joe and said in a small voice, "There's no way any more."

"You know, Billy," Joe said, standing up and stretching. He yawned. "You know, son, not long ago I was thinking about that time. I read this article in my detective magazine. This article was all about UFOs, you know, flying saucers. There were all these people, some folks in Iowa, a young fella in Kansas, an old lady and her old lady sister in Arizona, they all told about seeing these things. Funny thing ... big, round, white objects, they said, that came down like a star from out of the sky and hovered close above the ground. All these accounts, so strange, I thought, all so similar to each other and to my own experience. I've been wondering lately about it. Wouldn't that be something, now, if I saw an actual flying saucer?" He laughed slightly. "Might of been from Mars or somewhere. Imagine that, Billy, wouldn't that be something?" Joe turned around and walked back inside.

Billy felt like crying. He knew he'd have to go away. He'd tell Joe in the morning.

The dream that night was not like a dream. It seemed to Billy that he hadn't made the transition even, from sleep to waking in a dream. He was lying in bed unable to think much, not wanting to think much because he didn't want to worry or be afraid again. He heard a voice calling him. *Come here, boy. Get up, now, and come down here.* He got up from his bed and went outside. "*Hey, down here,*" the voice called. It was coming from down by the river. He went down there and walked along the edge, following the sound of the voice, which kept calling to him and urging him to hurry. At last he came to the place.

On the other side of the river was an old man.

He could see him plainly for there was a bright moon out. An old man with long white hair, dressed in buckskin. He smiled when he saw Billy, nodded and raised his hand in greeting. "Ahhhhhhh!" he said. Billy answered, "*Ahhhhhh!*" Waluwetsu. It was Waluwetsu and he could see again.

Waluwetsu motioned for Billy to cross over and join him. "No, I can't," Billy called, looking into the waters. "See here the river is too wide, too deep. The current is swift. I can't cross." He knew if he tried he would be pulled under and drowned. He thought he could walk along until he came to a place where the river was narrower. Waluwetsu turned his back and began to walk away. He walked slowly, stiffly, his thin, old body bent.

"Waluwetsu! Waluwetsu!" he called, "Waluwetsu, no!" But the old man kept walking, slowly, steadily, and would not turn. He went up into the hills and Billy could see him for a long time, a small, white figure moving slowly, until he was hidden among the trees.

It was still dark when Billy woke up. It was hard for him to realize, at first, that it had been only a dream.

Unable to sleep or rest he got up, then, and dressed and went downstairs. He built a fire and made a pot of coffee. He was sitting at the table looking out at the new day beginning when Joe got up. The coffee was ready now and the room filled with the delicate aroma. Joe brought their coffee in cups and sat down with him. Billy sipped his coffee slowly. Joe waited, his coffee still too hot. He held the cup and peered into the dark, steaming liquid.

"Dad," Billy said, "Dad, did you have a good sleep?" Joe nodded. "Dad, I gotta get away!" Joe

47

nodded again. He looked down at the table. An old oil cloth covered it. It had been white once, with blue and red and yellow paisley design. There were only a few places now where one could still see part of that faded design and the oilcloth was cracked and the white worn through to the brown. Where part of the design was left, Joe traced around and around with his finger. He nodded, his head bobbing heavily up and down. "Yeah, I guess so, son," he said. "I guess I kind of been expecting it, that you'd need to get away." And he looked into Billy's eyes. He picked up the steaming cup of coffee and brought it to his lips and blew on it, then sipped. "But," he said, "I thought maybe you'd be with me one more winter." Billy shook his head. "No, I can't. I'm sorry. I just got to get away, and."

"Yeah, I know." Then, "I'll write a letter to Alice Fay. I'll ask her if you can go to her. She'll say yes, I'm pretty sure."

"Alice Fay?" Alice Fay was Billy's half sister, Joe's daughter and his first wife's. Billy had only seen Alice Fay a few times in his life. She was years and years older than he was. She lived in a city along the coast.

"Alice Fay?" he asked.

"Where else, Bill? You got any ideas where else? *You*, you're still very young. It would be hard trying to make it on your own now."

"Yeah. But Alice Fay?" Billy said, "I guess so, huh?"

"I guess so, son."

It was a clear, cold day when Alice Fay's letter came a week or so later. The wind was blowing hard in high walls from the north and it was hard walking against it when Billy went to the mailbox to get it. The letter was addressed to him, to Mr.

48

Joseph William White Hawk, Jr. He stood with his back against the wind, his shoulders hunched, leaning into the wind and tore open the envelope. The handwriting was large, the letters rounded and legible, the lines rigidly straight. It said:

Dear Joseph William:

Our father wrote me, as I guess you know. He said you wanted to get away. He told me about Nicademus and Etta's boy, Tom, and how hard you are taking it. It was a terrible thing. Our dad doesn't want you to follow in Tom's footsteps, which, I happen to know, is the way of so many reservation boys. It was like that when I lived in the Benewah and it hasn't changed any. The Benewah is a terrible place to live. I was *so* fortunate to have gone away at a young age as I did and get a little education. I sympathize with you, Joseph. I sympathize with anyone who lives on that godforsaken piece of land. You can come. I want to help you get away. But one thing I want to impress upon you: I will not put up with any funny business. I work hard for what I have. I have a respectable, quiet life style. You must do nothing to ruin this. No drinking. No staying out all night or even staying out late. You will attend classes regularly. If you think you can live up to my requirements, then you are welcome to come. Remember, too, if you come and then don't do as I've asked, I can ship you right back there again. My other option is the state reformatory right here in this very city.

Your half sister,
Miss Alice Fay White

It was settled, then. He was getting away. He *was*. Alice Fay. Alice Fay? He laughed. *Alice Fay*.

He ran fast and hard, taking leaping steps. The wind, now traveling in the same direction as he, seemed to push him along, to lift him. He laughed and laughed and laughed, his mouth open wide, his head thrown back. He ran most all of the way home, until he was out of breath and his lungs ached and he could run no more. At last he fell down, his eyes closed tightly, his face pressed against the ground. He dug his fingers into the dirt, clutching. His heartbeat pounded in his chest and in his temples. He was sweating and the wind swept over him coldly. In all the world there were only the sounds of his gasping breathing, his heartbeat and the north wind.

CHAPTER V

It was a gray, cold morning. Billy was standing waiting for the westbound bus with his father by the road in front of the Bradley Cafe-Motel. Billy was glad of the new denim jacket he wore. He'd spent six dollars and ninety-five cents for the jacket at the dry-goods store out of the twenty-dollar bill Joe had given him that morning. His old one was, like the jeans he wore, thin and faded almost white and too short. Most all of his clothes were too small for him now, and his toes were crowded inside his scuffed, run-over-at-the-heels boots. He'd gone barefoot most of the summer and it was an odd feeling having the boots on again. His feet did not bend easily within them as he stepped.

"Here it comes," Joe said and pointed down the road at the bus. He looked at his wristwatch. "Ten minutes late." He reached in his back pocket and took out his billfold. He took Billy's bus ticket from the billfold and handed it to him. Billy took it and lifted the army duffel bag that had been Tom's off the ground and slung it over one shoulder. The bus was slowing down, getting ready to stop.

Billy turned to his father. They shook hands. "Be sure," his father said, "and write. Let me know how you're doing." Billy smiled. "Sure, Dad," he said, turning away. The bus stopped and its doors folded open. Billy ran and got on.

He found a place for himself near the back of the nearly empty bus. He lifted the duffel bag up onto the luggage space above his seat. It was not very heavy. He'd had very little to take along with him. He sat down.

The world outside became green-tinted as he looked through the bus's window glass. There was one-eyed Joe standing there still, watching the bus. Billy waved to him. Joe couldn't see him, though, behind the dark glass. Joe had made an occasion of this day. He'd shaved his face smooth and shiny and wet and oiled his hair and combed it back so that it lay down flat. He was wearing the eye patch and the old suit and a clean shirt, unbuttoned at the collar and without a tie. Billy smiled to himself, watching his father standing there, holding himself so straight, looking so clean and dressed up.

Billy, too, was freshly shaven, though he did not have a beard to shave. Along with the twenty-dollar bill Joe had given him a razor. He'd come into

Billy's room very early that morning, gently shaking him to wake him up, saying for him to get up as it was a big day, and when he was up and dressed Joe asked him casually, "Why don't you go to the truck? Look in the glove compartment."

When Billy was a little boy Joe would bring home candy and little toys, or pieces of fresh fruit and "hide" them in the glove compartment. That morning the treats were the twenty-dollar bill and the new razor. So, Billy lathered up his face and carefully scraped the lather off again with his new razor. Joe was pleased.

The door of the bus shut. The air brakes were released; a loud hissing followed. Then the bus pulled away from the Bradley Cafe-Motel leaving Joe standing there alongside the road.

Billy watched the dipping, rolling hills pass by. The yellow was yellow-green and the gray and brown were dull, gray-green. When the bus passed the hills and began climbing into the mountains the trees were dark, dark green. In the early afternoon the bus was near the summit and it was raining and dark as night.

Billy felt cramped. He shifted his weight one way, and then another. He pushed the button on the armrest that said RECLINE and made the back of the seat go back a little. He stretched out as best he could. He was conscious of his length. He would buy some new clothes for school with the money he had left, nice long clothes.

The heat came on inside the bus and it became very, very warm, Billy sat leaning his face against the cool window glass, his eyes closed, resting and listening to the loud, powerful motor and the splashing of the rain water underneath the tires and up against the bus.

In time, the bus passed the summit of the moun-

tain and for a few miles the narrow road seemed
almost level with only a gentle downward grade.
Then it was steep and the bus moved swiftly,
smoothly along down the western side of the
mountain. The air pressure lessened and Billy felt
his ears pop. The bus continued, going faster. The
rain stopped. It was warm enough again so that
the heat was not needed inside the bus and it was
turned off. They'd come all the way down now and
were no longer in the pass. It seemed quiet when
the noise of the heater subsided.

The bus came to a small town and passed
through. Then for maybe twenty miles there were
acres of farm land and some forested patches and
small houses sitting alongside the road or far back
in the fields in the darkness with just the squares of
light shining through windows. The houses would
be one or two or three miles apart.

Then the bus came to a freeway where there
were heavy traffic and lights above the road and
green highway signs and on the freeway the bus
passed by a small city. Near the freeway were the
outer edges of this city, power lines, filling stations,
realty businesses, only a few private homes. The
city itself was left behind but these outer edges
seemed to continue on and, the buildings for a mile
or two to become fewer. Then suddenly there were
many ... shopping centers, used car lots, flashy
billboard advertisements and Billy knew he'd
reached the outskirts of the big city, where Alice
Fay lived and where he was going to live.

There it was, he could see it now, still several
miles away, down low, it was, on the edge of the
sea. The road dipped and went around a sharp
curve and the main body of the city disappeared
behind a jutting hill, then came into view again.
The bus was heading down toward it, smooth and

fast, gliding like a powerful ship. Billy looked at the city lights and felt a strange excitement he'd not expected.

There was fog surrounding the city, but the fog was not so dense as to hide it. The lights were many and the buildings tall and close together where the lights shone, and the city lay sprawled upon steep hills. The city lights sparkled brightly in the night and lit the surrounding clouds of fog. The thin mist glowed white, tinted green through the window glass.

The bus drew nearer. It passed the city limits and entered into the city.

It was surprisingly lifeless for all the lights ... street lamps, they were, closed department stores with their window display lights on, office buildings with the windows of one or two floors lit up for night office workers. The moving neon lights turned out to be advertisements on billboards.

He saw one bar and then another. The beer signs in the windows were on and the name identifying the bar, but still, compared to the Big Bear Saloon these bars seemed lifeless and empty. Only here and there a person might be seen walking along the deserted, well-lit streets.

The depot was but ten blocks or so from where the freeway entered the town. It looked like a great, green, concrete barn with open air stables for the buses. It was across the street from the movie house that featured films the marquee claimed were for "mature adults only," *Motorcycle Chain Gang Girl* and *Tell It to Ruby*. The bus pulled into one of the open stalls and stopped and the bus driver announced into his microphone that everyone had to get off now because this bus wasn't going anywhere and those continuing on would have to transfer to another coach.

He'd gotten used to the green tint and it was a little startling when he left the bus and suddenly saw colors the way they were, and so bright. He had to blink his eyes in the sudden glare. People behind-him were shoving, moving, nudging, pushing to get away from the bus and out. It was impossible just to step aside and so he allowed himself to be pushed along with the crowd for a few feet.

The outer bus depot was like a huge shed. There was a roof overhead but no walls, just steel beams holding the roof up. On the far end was what looked like a small house with one big, glass window where a man with a microphone was announcing that the bus from Spokane had just arrived. Billy headed in the opposite direction of the announcer. He passed a glass cage where tanks of lemonade and grapeade and orangeade bubbled ... a group of game machines, Submarine Torpedo, Test Your Knowledge, Test Your Driving Skill, Test How Strong You Are, all huddled together in one corner near the four-chaired shoeshine stand. A young, red-haired, freckled baggage clerk stood behind the counter, elbows leaning on the counter, holding a book. Billy was going to smile at the baggage clerk if he looked up, but he didn't take his eyes off the book for a moment as Billy passed by.

At last he reached the main lobby. The walls were white, the floor was white (it was very dirty except for one small, roped off section near the quarter lockers where a middle-aged black man was mopping). The light was fluorescent, glaring, the kind of light that made you look tired and gray. Only one ticket window was open and he could see the agent there, too, was reading a book.

There were signs that told the arrival and departure times of buses and there were signs advertising hotel and motel accommodations, at reasonable rates, and tours and guide services and YMCA and Travelers Aid. A clock. He looked around for a clock. It was on the wall above the ticket office. It was late, he thought, nearly one. He hadn't checked the schedule but had reckoned it would be ten or thereabouts when he got in. Now he'd have to find Alice Fay. He spied a row of telephone booths along one wall.

He went over and set his duffel bag down on the floor, leaning against the booth, and went inside. He checked the directory (with some difficulty since he'd never done this before). Slowly and carefully turning the W pages. He could find no Alice Fay White Hawk listed. Nor could he find A.F. White Hawk, in fact, no White Hawk at all.

Then he remembered that he still had the letter she'd sent in his back jeans' pocket. He pulled it out and looked at it: Alice F. White the printed-on-gummed-paper return address said. So. Strange, he thought, he'd not noticed it before. Well, she'd not mentioned it in her letter; Joe didn't say anything about it. She'd dropped the Hawk from her name and became plain Alice F. White. Miss White, then. He stuck the envelope in his pocket and checked the directory once more. He found the name this time and dialed the number. After it rang about nine times a husky, soft, woman's voice answered, slow with the sleep still hanging on.

"Hmmmm. Who is this ... I don't know any ... wait a minute, oh, yeah ... *Billy*, Joseph William? Just a minute. Hold on, will you?" He waited maybe three minutes. When he heard her voice again it was more awake. "Hello? I'm sorry to keep you waiting but I needed to make myself wake up. I was afraid I might hang up and go back to sleep and forget you called afterward. Sometimes I do that. I forget things when I'm very sleepy or I imagine things, or dream them, you know. I mean, like once I'd parked my car across the street from my apartment in a tow-away zone. I set my alarm clock for ten minutes to five, you know, giving me ten minutes to get up and move my car to this side of the street. Well, the alarm went off and woke me up. I turned the alarm off and lay back down for just a second, you know, then of all things do you know what I did? I *dreamed* I got up and went downstairs and moved my car. Can you believe that? Oh, it seemed so real. When I woke up again an hour and a half later I actually believed I'd done it and I was *so* surprised when I went down and found it gone. At first I thought someone had stolen it but one of my neighbors, Mrs. Mobley, this sweet little old lady, you'll meet her, who lives upstairs, told me she'd seen it being towed away. So you see ... Ah, listen, you wait right there and I'll be down to get you, okay? Did you have a nice trip? How's Father?"

"Yeah, I had an okay trip. Rained in the mountains. Dad's well, he's okay. He's just fine."

"Good, I'll be right down. Bye." He heard the receiver click. He placed the phone back on the hook. He had no idea how far away from the terminal Alice Fay lived or how long it might take her to get there. He went outside and stood on the sidewalk in front of the depot. The street was deserted, even the mature adults' movie theater was dark now. He looked up and down. He went back inside.

There were not many people there, only a few sitting on benches looking tired or with their heads resting on their chests, dozing. There was a young blond woman with fine, tangled, wispy hair in a cotton print dress and a man's worn cardigan

57

sweater over it with holes in the elbows. She looked very white, sick-like, in fact. Billy thought, too, maybe she just looked that way because of the harsh light of the waiting room. The blond woman held a sleeping baby in her arms and there was another child sleeping with his legs curled up on the bench and his curly blond head resting on her lap. His face was dirty. There was a brown paper shopping bag on the floor near her and it had diapers and a baby bottle on top. She smiled tiredly when Billy walked past her and he returned her smile. There were dark circles under her eyes. He wondered how far she'd come and if she still had a distance to go.

He wandered back into the shed part of the depot where the pin ball machines and other game machines were. He looked at all of them, studied the directions. He went into a photomatic machine and took four little photos of himself, looking serious and intense, looking gay and abandoned, looking meanlike, the kind nobody better mess with. Yeah. Looking sad and lonely.

He stood around by the machine waiting for the photos to be developed. A red button of a light was on which meant, it said, that his photo was now being processed by a special method developed by Graphamatic, Inc. He could hear the insides of the machine groaning and whirring and grinding. Finally they emerged, a fresh, narrow strip, still wet and smelling funny. He held them carefully in the palm of his hand, not touching the surface with his fingers to avoid any smudging. He shook his head.

In each shot he looked almost exactly the same. In each his thick, dark hair hung down over his forehead just brushing his eyebrows and covered his ears and in each, the light from the picture-taking machine reflected too brightly in his eyes giving them a weird, madman gleam. He shook his head. Feeling foolish, he crumpled the still damp photos in his hand and took them over to the DEPOSIT LITTER HERE can and deposited them.

He went outside again and looked up and down the street. Still no sign. He went back inside. He sat down on the bench near the blond woman and her children. Over the loudspeaker it was announced that the south-bound San Francisco–Los Angeles coach was now boarding at Gate 16 and all but the woman and her children got up and left the waiting room.

Soon, a big, dark-haired man, dressed shabbily and looking like he needed a shave came into the waiting room and when the blond woman saw him she gave a little cry, "Jimmie." Her voice was high, "Jimmie, we're over here," and it had a decidedly southern sound. She was waving one hand at him. The baby stirred and tried to nuzzle up into her shoulder. The man came running over to her and bent down and took all three, the woman and the two children in his arms and held them. His face was deeply lined and weathered and Billy realized he was probably much younger than he appeared. The baby started crying and he had to let them go. The woman picked the baby up and put it over her shoulder and patted it and cooed, "Poor bybee," in her rounded southern speech and the baby quieted and slept again. The man carried the little boy and the brown paper shopping bag and the blond woman carried the baby and they left smiling, talking softly. Billy watched them leave. For five minutes he sat alone on the bench in the empty, white, harshly lit waiting room and he thought of those people, not in words he thought of them. He thought of the joy he'd seen in them and he knew how she'd tell him things like cute things the kids had done and he thought of them when they got home, how they'd turn out the lights and get into bed. The woman was tired. It would be so nice to rest. She'd nestle close to that man, he wondered how long they'd known each other, how long their marriage was. It would be so warm in their bed and he'd tell her how he'd missed her and they'd be so glad ... so glad. Foolish, foolish of Billy to sit thinking of such things.

He stood up and slung the duffel bag over his shoulder and went outside again. All the muscles in his body felt stiff and tired, aching. He turned up the collar of his denim jacket. It was so cold his breath made little clouds of fog and the cold was damp and heavy, not sharp like that morning in Idaho and it seemed to soak right through that jacket. In a few minutes he saw headlights way down the street. The car moved surely, evenly, not very fast. It was one of those big, powerful cars. It came nearer and nearer and then it stopped at the curb right in front of the depot. It was only a couple of years old, a Buick Special, all sparkle and shine, flaming persimmon in color. The woman driving the car had her hair in big, round, bristly rollers. She leaned over and opened the door for him. He walked over to the car.

"Just throw the bag in the back seat," she called. He opened the back door and threw the bag in, slammed it closed and climbed in the front seat with the woman in rollers he presumed to be Alice Fay. He knew she must be short because the seat was pushed up as near as it could go to the dashboard and he could not stretch his legs out comfortably. Alice Fay was smiling at him. She had a wide, full-lipped mouth and her teeth were very even and seemed extraordinarily white as they shone in the semi-darkness. Her eyes were not wide, just a little narrow and they slanted upward at the corners, almost orientally. Above her eyes were the sparsest pair of eyebrows Billy had ever seen, just two thin lines plucked into crescents. She was wearing bedroom slippers on her feet, the big, fluffy kind that looked like mops. She was, he guessed, thirty-five or more.

"Well," she said. "Well." He waited, confused. Her voice was pleasant, deep for a woman's voice, very deep and it was hoarse like she was just getting over a cold. "Well, fasten up your seat belt, boy. I insist whoever rides in my car must use the seat belt." He reached down and found the belt. He fumbled with it.

"Here. Let me show you," Alice Fay said, leaning over and reaching out her short, thick-fingered hands. "No," he said, pulling back. "What?" she asked, her hands still poised in the air, reaching. "I mean, you see there's no need," he laughed feebly. "I've got it okay now." He smiled at her. She put the car into drive and released the handbrake.

It was amazing, he thought, how the motor sounded. He could only hear it if he listened carefully and then it was like the purring of a big cat. So smooth. So much power. Alice Fay drove it up along a steep slope that went on for blocks and blocks. Away from the bus depot the streets were not so well lighted any more. Billy looked at Alice Fay. Her profile was illuminated by the dashboard fixtures. She had a high, round forehead, a small nose that turned up slightly on the end, then the full lips, a small, receding chin. She laughed, "Don't get scared of the way I look now without my make-up. *No* woman is at her best at two in the morning without make-up and with her hair in curlers. Don't worry." He laughed nervously ... or politely. Alice Fay seemed to let her laughter out easily, for emphasis, for punctuation. With him and with Joe and most people he knew it was not like that ... no one ever laughed without a reason. "This is a great car you got here," he said. She laughed again, a short, deep little laugh. "Yeah, it sure is, and if I keep up my payments it'll be all mine in less than a year." They came to the top of a hill and a yellow sign that said, STEEP GRADE USE LOW GEAR. She moved the automatic shifting device to low and then they were heading down a street so steep it seemed more a straight drop than a slope. They went very slowly and Alice Fay kept her foot on the brake. Billy was glad of the securely fastened seat belt. He clutched the armrest. "How about a little music?" Alice Fay asked and reached down and switched on the radio. Empty buzzing. She turned the dial trying to find a station that was still on the air but could find none. The street was long. They were heading toward the bay. "Is it very far?" Billy asked. "No," she answered, "we're almost there." He nodded. Good.

"This is sure a big city," he said quietly, awed, looking around on either side at the old, close together buildings and down in front of him where the long street ended and another section of the town began.

"No," Alice Fay laughed, "not so big, really. A hundred fifty thousand." A hundred fifty thousand, she said, and that it was not so big. Back home, he thought, back home Baker seemed like a huge, sprawling, busy city, that town seventy miles from Benewah. It was how big? Forty thousand? He looked out the window at the quiet, dark, deserted streets. He tried to imagine a hundred fifty thousand people. If all of them were standing crowded close together how many of these blocks would they fill.

"As cities go, it's not so big. Hah. Just wait until you see a big city . . . I mean like L.A."

"Really? L.A.? You been there?"

She nodded. "Yeah. I been there all right. That's where the BIA sent me to learn how to operate my machine. Lived there a year. Wild." She'd gone through the Bureau of Indian Affairs educational channels. Relocation was what they called it. Designed, as the president said, "to draw the Indian into the mainstream of American life."

He knew all about relocation. He knew enough people who went away on it. They sent you away to some city place, never near your home, but a long ways away. There you took some kind of vocational course and they gave you thirty dollars to live on a week until you'd completed their course. Then they gave you thirty dollars a week to live on while you looked for work for eight weeks. After that they cut you loose.

"I've thought," he said, clearing his throat, "I've thought of taking relocation. Taking something like machinist, welder, something like that." Actually he hadn't given it any thought, not until just then when Alice Fay brought it up. He knew you had to be at least eighteen, though, and you had to be living on a reservation in order to apply. Sometimes it took a long time before it came through. Clara, Tom's sister had to wait two years to take her secretary course. Then she couldn't find a job nearby so she just stayed home to wait until something came up.

"Oh, yeah," she said. "Aw, you can do better than *that*." She yawned, big and long, as if she were enjoying her yawn. "Excuse me," she said. And seeing her had made Billy yawn too, and then he had to say "Excuse me," too, as she had done to be polite. They'd entered into an old neighborhood where there were a lot of bars and shabby-looking, unpainted buildings and the streets were narrow. "We're almost home, Bill," she told him. She turned into a dark alleyway and at the end turned to the right and parked at the corner in front of a little bar named ARNIE'S HIDEAWAY. She turned off the engine and withdrew the key from the ignition and put it in her coat pocket. "Here we are," she said. "Home sweet home." "Here?" He nodded. "You live in a bar?" "No." She laughed. "Up there." There was an apartment building above Arnie's and above the dirty-windowed cafe a few doors down.

Alice Fay unlocked the front door and pushed it open. Billy followed her and was standing behind her and just inside the door as she turned and pulled the key and finally loosened it and worked it free from the lock. She pushed a button on the wall near the door and a dim light came on. "Well, how do you like it?" Alice Fay laughed. The walls of the foyer were pink plaster, cracked and stained. An empty wine bottle lay on the concrete floor. It smelled old and musty like air from the outside had not been in there in a long time and it smelled like fresh catshit.

Alice Fay motioned for him to begin climbing the stairs. "The second floor, apartment B, the first door to your left across the hall from the garbage chute." He nodded and uncertainly started up the stairs. Alice Fay followed, her muffy slippered footsteps noiseless, jingling the keys inside her coat pocket.

Alice Fay's apartment was small and fastidiously clean. The floors of her three rooms were scrubbed spotless and waxed and polished to a smooth, glossy finish. All through the apartment, almost killing the old, musty odor, was the smell of Lysol disinfectant. (She mopped up every single day, he found out, and gave the place a thorough cleaning, window washing, old wax removed and new applied every Saturday, just like she'd been taught at the BIA school.) And, looking around the apartment, he could not see a thing lying about casually, without plan—all surfaces were cleared and dusted. There were no curtains at the windows, only plain, tan blinds. The walls were painted white. Alice Fay had done the painting herself, she told him. When she moved in the walls were positively filthy, a sickly green-brown color. It was, if not severe, then very plain, without decoration, and without sign of there being a person living here. It was like a furnished, vacant, newly cleaned apartment on display for prospective tenants. Alice Fay told him she paid one hundred and ninety dollars a month for the apartment, half her take-home pay.

"I found out later why they let it go so cheap ... little Annie upstairs told me. There was a big, jagged hole in the glass of my door when I first moved in. I'd just gotten out of the shower and was stark naked when this grubby little hand came through that hole. I yelled, 'Hey, cut that out,' but that little hand reached right down and turned the knob and opened the door. I yelled at her to get out but the little creep just stood there staring at me. I picked up a shampoo tube and threw it at her and she ducked out. I got dressed and went looking for her. Her mother, Mrs. Quinch, she's a creep too, an even *bigger* creep, said she sent Annie down to find out if Clotille was back. 'Who's Clotille?' I asked. Dumb Mrs. Quinch smiled, you know, *evasively* and rolled her eyes at Annie like they were hiding something and Annie tittered, holding her hand covering her mouth. 'Clotille was, the ah, previous tenant,' she said. Annie tittered again. I left then. A few days later Annie came down by herself and told me Clotille was a prostitute and her mother had called the cops on her and had her taken away. It was the cops that broke the window glass, she said, because Clotille wouldn't let them in. Mrs. Quinch wanted Annie to find out if Clotille had left her little poodle dog behind and that was what she was doing there, that day when I just got out of the shower. The damn dumb Mrs. Quinch. She's sickly, she claims. Stays in bed all the time. *Her boy friend* is a huge, big-bellied negro. So anyway, when I first moved in, there were all these guys ringing my doorbell, all hours. I'd stick my head out the window and call down and ask what they wanted. Most of 'em just said, sorry, wrong address and went away. Once this guy asked me if I was a 'dancer' like Clotille. Ha ha. Look. Look at this"—she took him and showed him in her bedroom on the carpet on both sides of the bed, dozens and dozens of little, black, round cigarette holes burned through—"I'd like to tear the carpet up but the landlord won't let me. I *did* tear it up in the living room, though. It was the same way in there." Then, "You know, it's funny, I mean a prostitute living in a place like this. I mean I always thought they either lived in brothels, you know, or else in fancy penthouses. Annie said Clotille was fat and had fuzzy red hair." She shook her head.

Billy wondered why Alice Fay had never married. He wondered why she worked so hard cleaning and recleaning the way she did.

CHAPTER VI

When Billy had been with Alice Fay ten days, he had a birthday. He became fifteen years old. He hadn't meant to remember. It meant nothing, he told himself, yet he did remember. He was aware of the date because school would be starting in a few days, that was it, not because of his birthday.

He woke up in the misty cold morning to the usual Alice Fay noises: her padding footsteps in her room and in the bathroom, the shower running, gargling.

Usually the disturbance was temporary. Billy wouldn't open his eyes at all but lie still and relaxed until she left and it was quiet again and he could gently ease back into his sleep. He was wide awake this morning. It should be different somehow today, he thought, he should do something to make it different.

Billy heard the sharp click click click of high-heel shoes, the door open and shut. She was gone.

Billy slept on the davenport in the living room. It was narrow and not quite long enough so that he had to sleep either with his knees drawn up or his ankles propped up on the arm of the davenport. He could feel the springs pushing hard and metallic against his body and while the first few nights it had been almost impossible to sleep upon, he'd gotten used to it, in a way.

He was lying with his face pressed against the back of the davenport now, the covers up high over his shoulders. He turned over. He threw the covers back and got up, yawned, stretched, pulled on his Levi's, put on the shirt that had holes in the elbows and was frayed around the collar and cuffs. He needed new clothes. He hated to ask Alice Fay and he hated to write Joe to send more money. The twenty dollars Joe had given him had somehow dwindled to eighty-five cents and he'd not bought anything with it besides the Levi jacket he got in Bradley the day he left. The rest he'd spent on comic books and candy bars and a few packs of cigarettes, though he was not a regular smoker, actually.

He went into the kitchen barefoot and put the tea kettle on the stove, turned the dial on and, pouring a little instant coffee into a cup, sat down and waited until the tea kettle whistled. He switched the dial and poured the boiling water into the cup. He wondered what Joe would be doing now. It would probably be cold there and Joe would have to build a fire in the mornings. Would he remember to keep kindling in the woodbox? Would he be in enough control to keep himself well and alive when it got so cold? He remembered how several men he knew had been found frozen to death in the snow within feet of their homes, passed out drunk. He tried his coffee too quickly and it burned the tip of his tongue. He blew on it. Joe would be all right, though, he thought. He knows how to take care of himself. He sipped his coffee. He'd tried to write Joe a letter once but he hadn't known what to say besides how are you doing, I'm doing all right myself.

Yeah, he'd been doing all right, hanging around Alice Fay's apartment all day long, watching out the window, staring into space, at the blank, white

68

walls and the face of the electric clock while the red second needle swept the time away. He napped a lot. He went to the store a block away and bought candy bars and cigarettes and comic books. He liked the thrillers, the kind with mutant-like heroes battling on the side of justice. Twice he'd bought a strange newspaper full of bizarre events. (What had first attracted his attention was a headline: MAN CLAIMS, "MY WIFE WAS TOO TALL SO I CUT OFF HER FEET.") He'd thrown the papers down the garbage chute before Alice Fay returned from work. She even disapproved of the comic books, calling them cheap trash and saying they were going to cause his mind to rot. She urged that he apply to go to BIA school. "They'd straighten you out, Bill," she said, "*fast*." Then she laughed and added, "I don't know though, actually. You're already mostly grown. Bad habits already established. I don't know if they'd be able to do much with you, actually. Ah, well." And went back to her TV watching.

Alice Fay was a great prime-time TV viewer. In the evenings she liked to sip a little sherry while she watched TV. Those were her words, "sipping a little sherry." In an evening's time she would kill a whole fifth "to unwind a bit after a hard day. To relax, not to get drunk and throw myself around and be an ass like those dirty reservation Indians." By the time the late movie had ended, though, Alice Fay had to try very hard to walk straight when she got up to go in to bed, but didn't quite make it. It was not every evening, just two or three times a week.

Billy, too, was a TV fan. Every day he watched the midday movie. They played a game on the program called "Dialing for Dollars," where they played a record, then at random chose a name out of the telephone directory and asked whoever answered to identify the name of the song they were playing. If they were able to identify it correctly, they would win the money in the jackpot. Nobody had won in a long time now and over one thousand dollars had been accumulated. Each day a little more was added. Billy kept hoping that some day they'd call him and he'd guess lucky and win and get all that money. He'd sit and watch the movie and the "Dialing for Dollars" and listen to the records and make up possible titles ... "Ocean Breezes," "The Summer Days," "All My Love." Just anything might be right. And he'd daydream of what he'd buy with his winnings, new clothes for himself. He'd give Alice Fay a couple of hundred. Boy, would she be surprised. "Here's a little something to help out with the groceries and rent," he'd say nonchalantly. Hah. He could just see the look on her face. And he'd buy Joe something too. A coat. A nice, new, warm, expensive coat. Green maybe. The coat would be green, yes, and have a hood and a heavy pile lining. It would be beautiful. The coat Joe had now he'd had for a long time. He'd bought it at the Goodwill in Spokane one winter and it had never been cleaned. It was shabby-looking, long and black, *too* long, coming past his knees and the sleeves way down to the middle of his hands. When it was cold he wore it with the collar turned up. There were a lot of stains on the coat, and white, dusty lint. Maybe he'd buy Joe something really nice too, like one of those little transistor TV sets.

But Dialing for Dollars never called Billy and he never had a chance to win the jackpot. Today he wouldn't watch. It would be just his luck, he thought if they called today while I'm out.

In the apartment next door it sounded like someone was moving furniture back and forth across their floor. Somewhere an angry baby's cry, loud and frantic. Abruptly the cry stopped. Upstairs the organ music began. It seemed too early for old Mrs. Mobley to be at it, but she was.

Mrs. Mobley and Alice Fay were friendly. Mrs. Mobley was a widow and lived alone. She was very religious, he knew, since she gave Alice Fay funny little coloring pictures depicting some Bible story or another from her church's Sunday school. "For your little brother," she said. "When you are eighty," Alice Fay explained, "most everyone must seem like a child." He had one of Daniel in the lions' den and one of Jesus suffering the little children to come unto him and one of Baby Jesus and Mary. He read the texts on the backs of the pictures and he probably would have colored them if he'd had crayons. There seemed very little to do.

Mrs. Mobley was quite deaf even with the large hearing aid she wore and one had to speak loudly to her.

Mrs. Mobley was singing. She had a very loud, strong voice, surprising for a woman so old and frail. She was accompanying herself on the electric organ. She sang in the wrong key: "Rock of Ages." He heard the wretched Mrs. Quinch who lived next door to Mrs. Mobley thumping something, a broom, maybe, against the wall and yelling in her ugly, nasal voice, "Quiet, quiet in there you old bat, or I'll call the cops on you. Have you arrested for disturbing the peace." The day had begun.

He put the coffee cup in the sink and started out of the kitchen, then stopped and went back and washed it and wiped it dry and replaced it neatly in the cupboard. Alice Fay had gotten very angry with him once when she came home and found dirty dishes sitting in the sink, so angry she almost turned purple and it took her a long time to calm down all the way and get back to normal. He was afraid she'd make him go home. "Just like one of those dirty Indians everyone's always hearing about," she'd ranted, "is it any wonder ... dirty Indians living in filth and squalor and then they wonder why *they* think we're not as good as them!" She was a fanatic, it seemed, on keeping herself, and now Billy, too, a clean Indian just like she'd learned in BIA school. It was as though Alice Fay's official slogan was, "The only good Indian is a dead Indian ... *or a clean one* ..."

He went back into the living room and folded his bedding and put it up on a shelf in the closet.

The davenport was under two long windows and just outside these windows was the fire escape landing. He liked to go out there, especially in the afternoons when the sunlight came around there, and sit with his arms hooked through the railing bars and his legs dangling in space above the street and watch and listen. He climbed out on the fire escape now, even though it was in shadows and not warm. Arnie was sweeping up around the door of Arnie's Hideaway, getting ready to open up. He looked up and saw Billy and waved and smiled and Billy waved and smiled back. The sky was clear of fog now, a deep, dark blue and sheets of thin, white clouds floated westward, out toward the open sea.

He watched the Kweauss children playing across the street in the sun and in the alleyway alongside. They were running and playing, laughing and shouting. Two little girls were jumping rope together and chanting a rope-jumping ditty. The street was dirty and littered and there were pieces of broken glass glittering in the bright sunlight. A dog yapping a bark, and then there appeared two dogs running alongside one another, a big hairy one and a little skinny-looking one with hardly any hair and pointed ears that stood straight up.

There were winos who lived in that neighborhood. They slept on the street, in doorways, covering themselves with newspapers for warmth. They had no home but they always stayed within the same two blocks. This morning there was a group of these men sitting together in a patch of sunlight down the street. They were sitting on the edge of the curb near a place where street repairs had been going on and the area marked off with tall pink-orange fluorescent cones, standing in a long row. One of the winos was wearing a street-repair cone on his head. Billy smiled when he saw him. It looked gay—a tall, orange pointy party hat, bobbing up and down, moving from side to side as the man talked animatedly with his companions.

By God, Billy thought, another thing I'm going to do when I get all that "Dialing for Dollars" money is buy those guys some fancy wine, a whole case of it, imported from France maybe. He'd bring it down to them nice and chilly and there'd be red ribbons tied around the necks of the bottles. He laughed out loud at the thought.

He sat out there on the fire escape with his legs dangling over the edge until he heard the loud notes start up down in Arnie's Hideaway. That meant it was ten-thirty at least. He climbed back through the window. He closed it and locked it behind him. Alice Fay said a man came in the window once when she first moved in and took her steam iron and electric mixer and record player. That was before she got the television.

Billy sat on the davenport and pulled on his socks that needed mending and his boots over them. Inside the apartment, with the windows

73

closed, the notes of the jukebox were not rich and clear. All you could hear was the monotonous bass keeping time and it was so loud you could feel the floor vibrate when you put your fingers lightly upon it.

He wondered for just a moment where he'd go, what he would enjoy doing. It didn't matter, really, he decided. It didn't matter enough to wonder about and plan and go through all that. He checked the pocket for the keys Alice Fay had given him. They were not there. He got down on his hands and knees and looked under the davenport. Then in the bathroom. He could think of no place else. The apartment was so neat that nothing could be lost under undisturbed rubble like when he lived at home with Joe. He considered not going. No, he had to go, though. He left, locking the door behind himself.

For all the hours he'd spent watching the street from the fire escape he'd not gone out there many times, only to the laundromat with Alice Fay and shopping for groceries with Alice Fay and to the little store on the corner to spend his money. From up on the fire escape he'd gotten used, in a way, to Alice Fay's neighborhood and it was often very pleasant and interesting. It was not the same, though, once he found himself locked outside the apartment house doors and standing in the street. Now he was right down in it, not just watching, passing the hours away, musing, from a nice, safe distance. He didn't know which direction to begin walking. Arnie's Hideaway's doors were open to the warm morning. Inside he could see only Arnie and another man. The odor was strong—urine, cigar smoke, stale air. He crossed the street. The children playing there stopped and became quiet and watched him pass with their faces somber and closed. He could not hear them when he passed. He looked back over his shoulder and saw them still watching. The whites of their eyes were startlingly white in the black faces. One little boy, his eyes narrowed, gestured obscenely at Billy. "What-choo lookin' at nigga?" the boy said. Billy quit looking. The boy seemed to be no more than nine or ten, a small, scrawny nine or ten. Kweausses. Black people. He'd observed them among themselves, the ones on his street, always laughing, making jokes among themselves. The children fought a lot sometimes but later they seemed to have forgotten about it. He remembered how one day he'd seen one of those bums, lying in a wino-stupor, getting beaten and kicked by Kweauss children who'd run away when Arnie saw them and yelled. He shuddered. They were everywhere. Black, yellow. Big, white teeth and pink gums. He'd never seen a black person up close before except for young Midnight, who'd spent one year in Bradley and been in his fourth-grade class. He took long steps and moved as quickly as he could without appearing to be running away.

For a few blocks he was deep into the heart of Kweauss section, he walked along the main drag. There were bars, Willie's and Black & Tan, Bourbon Beat, boarded up store fronts with the words, SOCIAL CLUB, painted above the doors. A Muslim mosque. Young men walking along in beards and woolly, fuzzy natural hair so wide he wondered how they got through doorways, wearing loose, buttonless, wide-sleeved African print shirts. Older men in shabby clothes, not quite like the bums that slept in the streets near Alice Fay's, but still obviously men with nothing to do, no involvement, outside hanging around together in front of Willie's or the Barbecue Pit. There were dime stores and department stores and all had dummies that looked just like other dummies except that they were painted a dark color and wore black, fuzzy wigs. Two young women walked hurriedly along the street, their eyes aimed straight ahead. They were well-dressed Kweauss women, the heels of their polished shoes medium height. The men hanging around called to them, "Hey, pretty, where you goin' in such a hurry?" "Oooo-eee," and made obscene remarks about the physical endowments of the young women. "Hey, Mamma, can I walk wit' you?" one man in wrinkled clothes with rotten teeth asked and walked along beside them and tried to get them to talk. The women ignored all this, keeping their eyes aimed straight ahead, their expressions frozen, revealing nothing, as if they were very used to this kind of thing. Billy thought they must work around here in an office or something, maybe even live here.

He came to the end of the Kweauss district. It was small, just a few blocks really, the main street maybe seven blocks altogether. When he crossed the street there were doctors' offices and a big, brick building with a revolving red-and-white sign that advertised that this was the credit dentist's building. EASY TERMS. Then there were apartment buildings, Kweauss still, but much better kept than the others, much more expensive. He walked to the top of the steep, concrete covered hill, then began down again. He came to a restaurant that had a menu in its window that showed it was possible to buy a dinner for nine dollars inside and he knew he'd come to another section of town. His toes ached inside the tight boots.

He wandered around aimlessly for hours, his feet aching, wondering where he might go. He went to two department stores and rode the escalators up and down. It was unpleasant seeing the tight, hostile faces of the shoppers.

Billy went outside and walked in the general direction of the apartment, slowly, tiredly.

He found a park and took off his boots and socks and carried them while he walked and felt the cool, damp grass beneath his feet. He sat under a tree with many branches that grew out wide away from the tree, luxurious branches with full yellow and brown and still-green leaves and he leaned his back and his head against the thick, rough-barked trunk of that tree and rested.

He came to the museum when he began walking home again. It was a two-story white stucco building at the edge of the park with large windows washed so clean it might look as though there were no glass there at all except the glass caught the reflections. He'd been to a museum once. His sixth-grade class in Bradley, along with Mrs. Dailey's fifth graders had chartered a bus and gone on a field trip to the county seat. They took their lunches along in paper bags and sang silly songs on the way and played around so much teacher had the driver stop once so she could chide them and make them behave like ladies and gentlemen. They'd gone to a museum. He didn't remember it too well, the museum itself, but he remembered going there and he remembered he'd enjoyed that day so much. He walked up the clean, white steps and opened the museum door. The door was big and heavy and it moved slowly and silently.

It was quiet inside, very, very quiet and not warm enough somehow. The front room was large, the floors smooth and shiny, a floor Alice Fay would envy. There were tall, leafy, potted plants standing near the wall near doors that went into the other rooms of the museum.

There was an old woman with silver hair sitting behind a counter reading a book. She was a well-cared-for old woman, dressed in an expensive green wool dress, her nails carefully, flawlessly manicured. Her silver-tinted hair was done in graceful, deliberate waves. Her features were calm and serene. She glanced up at him briefly over the rims of her glasses and smiled sweetly, then resumed her reading. There were souvenirs, key chains, ash trays with pictures of the museum painted on them, postcards and little booklets for sale at the old woman's counter in the display case. He went through one door, stepping carefully. His footsteps seemed loud in that big, empty, quiet place.

The museum was full of pioneer things, as it turned out, reminders of a tough and glorious past. There was an old restored covered wagon complete with water barrels, cooking utensils and the like fastened to its side. It was behind velvet ropes. A little typewritten sign warned not to touch and said the wagon had belonged to a man named Jeremiah McCloud and he'd come all the way from Missouri in the wagon. A wax likeness of old Jeremiah sat on the wagon's board, holding reins in his hand. The likeness had bright, courageous glass eyes and a strong, jutting chin.

There were rifles and pistols, shooting irons, crude, handmade tools for working the soil. One room was made up to look like a genuine pioneer cabin with a spinning wheel and a loom, a homemade bed covered with a patch quilt.

Billy was not interested in these things. He saw a sign that said UPSTAIRS OPEN TODAY UNTIL 5:00 and he went on up there.

He found, first of all, the buckskin-clad, coon-skin-capped wax figures of Lewis and Clark. Sacajawea in her fringed buckskin dress was standing just in front of them. She had a baby strapped to her back in its cradle board. They were looking out over a papier-mâché landscape of hills and forest and bay, shading their eyes with their hands from a sun that was not there. It was supposed to depict the moment they first saw the site where the city was later built. Billy watched them a moment. Such serious expressions on the wax faces, and the red, feverish cheeks, the too delicate features, the relentless, glassy stares. They'd come a long way.

He was almost ready to leave, finding nothing but the relics of the city's early days, when he came into a small, inner room lit only by the lights inside the display cases.

He did not see *it* at first lying there in the middle of the small room. He saw the strangeness, though, the abrupt change—the lack of frontier-day relics. It was a different feeling.

The mummy's face and hands were exposed. Where the face was exposed it appeared intentional, as though who'd ever prepared him for display had undone the wrapping and made it like that. Where the hands were exposed, though, the wrappings had decayed and worn away. Billy was standing right over looking down at the mummy.

Attached to the mummy's glass display case was a little typewritten index card. It informed whomever it might concern that this mummy was approximately two thousand years old and he'd been from the upper class but he was no one very rich. He was no one of any real importance. The mummy was just an ordinary guy. They had all these things they'd taken from his tomb and things they'd found buried in the ruins of other tombs, little statues, intricately carved, and pieces of jewelry, earthen pottery and things to eat with. It said on a larger card how the ancient Egyptians had put those possessions in with the mummified dead when they sealed their burial places because it was part of their religion. They believed the mummy's spirit would need those things on his long journey and later when he arrived in the other world.

He kept looking at the mummy's gray face. You could see teeth where the lips had eroded away, little brownish, pointy teeth, and there was a little hair still left, faded a reddish brown, on his poor, small, and shrunken mummy's head.

He lowered himself and sat cross-legged on the floor near the mummy's case and thought of two thousand years. He tried to consider the passage of those years, to remember how long a year was, then two, then three—eventually there would be two thousand, somewhere way, way back. He wondered what this man's name had been, how he'd lived his life and how he'd ended it, what made him angry and what made him glad? A man, the mummy lying here, had been a man living two thousand years ago, yet much of him remained still for Billy to look upon, lying there all shriveled, gray and ancient under the lit glass display case. The thought was overwhelming. The thought was calming.

A man in a blue uniform and a police-like cap passed by the mummy's door. In a few minutes he returned. He stopped this time and stuck his head in the door. He had a badge that said Special something on it. He could not make out the other word, curving around the bottom of the badge—it was done in much smaller letters. The man looked around, checking, suspicious. He went away, then returned in a few minutes. Billy had to leave then because the man said he was going to close up.

Outside, a strong, fast-moving wind had come up

and it was brisk. He wore only the thin, worn, red-plaid shirt, no jacket, no undershirt underneath, and the wind seemed very cold to him. He wondered how it was in Benewah right now. Certainly he would not be out walking around with no jacket on.

He thought of the Benewah winters he'd known all his life, the blizzards and the driving snow, the bitter coldness, the dulling monotony of the days when the whole country lay snowbound and frozen. The first snow was exciting. Each year it was a good thing to wake up and find snow on the ground, he liked playing in the snow and making things out of it, walking in it ... for a while, then soon tired of it all and longed for the springtime again. Here there would be no snow. Alice Fay said sometimes, once in a while there might be a little, just two inches or three and it would stay on the ground a few nights then the rain would come and melt it away. There was a great deal of rain, she said, in these winters.

When he was almost home a Kweauss woman in skinny high-heel shoes and suede coat with a fur collar stopped him, touching his arm lightly. She was a rich, cocoa brown, and her lips were painted orange and she was wearing a shoulder-length, loose, banged blond wig. She leaned close to him and whispering, asked him if he would like to have a party. He could smell mint on her breath. He'd never heard the term she used, having a party, yet he understood. He told her all he had was eighty-five cents and she shrugged disgustedly and took her hand away from his arm.

CHAPTER VII

Joe once told Billy about the time he first saw a Kweauss.

Joe was a boy then, nine or ten years old. Some Suyappi prisoners had escaped from the fort and were hiding in the woods and Joe and some other boys were watching them, those two prisoners. The boys were quiet and never got too close to them. They'd not seen a great many Suyappi in their lives. Each day the boys would come to the place where the prisoners had made camp and watch them more. One day a group of soldiers came looking for those men and they found them and they chased them through the woods and captured them. The soldiers were Kweauss and none of the boys had even heard of a Kweauss. As the soldiers were taking the prisoners back the boys followed along, unseen, hidden in the bushes and trees. Fascinated they came nearer and nearer until they could clearly hear the voices of the men and clearly see their faces.

One of the soldiers was tall, Joe said, a giant, almost seven feet and black and shiny. The tall soldier was following behind one of the prisoners and when the prisoner would slow down or turn his head around the black shiny soldier would poke him or threaten him with his bayonet and in his deep, rich voice say, "Get along dere, boy." The boys were delighted. It was the first English words Joe had ever heard and remembered.

Joe and his friends, then, would play a game of the prisoners and soldiers and take turns being the tall, black shiny one. Everybody wanted to be that one because he got to poke the ones who were the prisoners with a stick and command them in a deep, southern voice, "Get along dere, boy," words they would not know the meaning of for years to come.

Lincoln Junior High was housed in a big square slab of gray concrete. Above the entrance, engraved, were the words, AND THE TRUTH SHALL MAKE YOU FREE. Inside was a milling, squirming, noisy sea of humanity, almost all black. He saw a doorway marked office down the hall and he proceeded to push and wind his way through the crowd. He smelled that salty-sour odor of perspiration. It was them, the Kweausses. They had that way of smelling too, just like the Suyappi had. It was overwhelming in the crowded, unventilated hallway.

When he got to the office he had to wait in line to see a secretary. When he finally got to her she gave him a card and said his counselor's name was Mr. Hughes and she showed him where he could wait. It was the counselor's outer office.

There were three or four chairs in the outer office and these were taken. Ten or more people were standing. He watched the wall clock until five minutes had gone by. He leaned against the wall, holding his spiral notebook and watched the clock. He listened to the voices of the other waiters. Strange, it was, the way they talked. "He do, and then she say. Rilly! it look okay. She gonna ax fo it.

Boss. Bad." By noon only five of them had been seen by the counselor. During the noon hour no one was seen. Billy got hungry. One o'clock came and he was still waiting in the outer office.

It was well into the afternoon, almost time for school to let out when he finally got in to see Mr. Hughes. Mr. Hughes was a cigar smoker and his office was filled with stale smoke.

"Hello there, young fellow," the man said, extending one small, smooth, hand to Billy. "I'm Ed Hughes, your counselor this year." Billy took his hand. It was soft and fragile: a woman's hand, and they shook hands feebly. Mr. Hughes's palm was wet and clammy and Billy wiped his hand on his jeans when the handshake was finished.

"Sit down, my boy," Mr. Hughes said, indicating one of the two straight-backed chairs, the one closest to the desk. He was a slight, round-shouldered man with a long, narrow head and his colorless brown-gray hair was thinning on top. He had a long blue piece of paper on his desk with a list of names. Alongside most of them, on the left hand side, he'd marked a check with his red pen. There were only a few, five or six or so, names left.

Mr. Hughes was looking down at the list on the long blue piece of paper, running his finger down along the names. Billy sat down and waited.

A loud buzzer sounded somewhere, and then there was a lot of noise, shouting, laughing, footsteps, metal locker doors clanging. The noises rang and echoed through the halls, each blending with the others, becoming distorted; a strange, crazy din. Mr. Hughes lifted his wrist to his face and checked his watch. Annoyed, he shook his head and muttered something to himself.

"Now, then, young fellow, you must be David Blaine, right?" He had his finger next to one of the names on the sheet of paper and he was looking at Billy and smiling. Mr. Hughes sounded like he needed badly to clear his throat but it must have just sounded like that because it didn't seem to bother him. It was irritating. Billy cleared his own throat. "No, sir," he answered, "I'm not David Blaine ..." "Wait!" Mr. Hughes raised one hand like a traffic cop directing traffic to stop. "Wait a minute!" He made a little note alongside the name he'd had his finger on a moment before, David Blaine's name, Billy guessed. "What's going on here? You're *supposed* to be David Blaine." He was checking his list and looking in the little gray metal card file that was sitting on his desk.

Behind Mr. Hughes's desk was a big window and Billy was watching the people out there in the cement-covered, fenced-in playing court. They were standing around in groups, shooting baskets, just walking along on their way out. He noticed most had big, wooly Afro hair and flowing, African print shirts and dresses, toga-like dresses. (Not like where *he* came from.) He was wearing a red western-style shirt Alice Fay had bought. He looked down at his cracked, faded, ugly boots and thought of them in contrast to the Kweauss boys' shoes, so shiny, they were, and smooth. They looked like they were made of smooth, black or brown glass. He wondered how he'd look with a big, woolly, bush of hair and an African shirt. Ridiculous! He smiled.

"Okay," Mr. Hughes said, "I think I got this thing straightened out, now. You're Henry Willats." Billy could see how tired and irritated Mr. Hughes was. He almost wished he *were* Henry Willats so he and Mr. Hughes could both get out of there and go home. "No, sir, I'm sorry," he said, "but I'm not

Henry Willats, either." His long face was pale and lined.

"Okay." He sighed. *"Who are you?"*

"My name is Billy White Hawk, sir."

Mr. Hughes looked down at his list, skimmed his finger down and up and down again, squinting his eyes, muttering, "Wyedock, Wyedock, Wyedock. How do you spell that name, kid?" Billy told him.

"White Hawk? Oh really? Say, are you a, an a ..."

"I'm an American Indian."

Mr. Hughes nodded and smiled. "Oh, how interesting. My great-grandmother was a Cherokee ..." He seemed to be waiting for a response. After a moment he checked his list again.

"No, sorry, it's not here," he said. "Are you sure you're supposed to go to this school and not Jason Lee or Franklin? All are in close proximity. The boundaries sometimes overlap."

"Yes, sir, my sister called up the board of education and found out for sure. I'm supposed to go to Lincoln."

"I don't know how come your name's not on the list then. Who told you I was to be your counselor?" Billy wished he would clear his throat.

"You did, Mr. Hughes. When I came in here you said ..."

"No, no, I mean before. Who sent you to me?"

"The main office. They told me to come in here when I first came in this morning. I waited in the outer office all day. I didn't even go to lunch."

"Did you come in during the third week of August and register like you were supposed to do?" Billy shook his head no.

"Well, you should have, you know." He shook his head, leaned back and pressed his eyes with his fingers. Then sat straight. "Ah well. Tomorrow you go back to the main office and tell them there you never registered. They'll take care of you. And so you won't have to come back here again, let me tell you what I'm supposed to tell you right now, okay?" He took a deep breath and leaned far back in his chair, pushing it away from his desk. He propped his feet up on the desk and crossed them. His socks didn't match. One was long and black and disappeared up under his pants leg, the other short and brown and revealed about two inches of pale, white flesh between sock and pants, flesh much whiter than his hands or face. There were two round holes worn in the bottoms of his shoes. He began talking in a monotonous, singsong voice, like he'd repeated many times his counselor's speech.

"First of all, let me tell you we have three levels of academic achievement here at the school: level A, level B, level C. You will be placed at level B and you will remain at level B unless you do outstanding work in which case you will be promoted to A, or if you fail, be demoted to level C. Did I make myself clear?" Billy nodded. "There are two sessions: seven-thirty to three, and nine-thirty to five. You will be in the latter."

"All right, then. Now"—at least he cleared his throat and the scratchiness disappeared—"adolescence, my boy, is a difficult time of life for anyone. It's a period of rapid, and often times confusing, changes. You're no longer a kid, not yet an adult. Very difficult. Hormones play a vital role too. We realize that here and we do our best to understand." He smiled. "Why, believe it or not, I was once an adolescent myself," and he chuckled. "So, I am here to help and guide you over any rough spots you may encounter. If you need someone to talk things over with, uh, uh," he groped for his name. He glanced at a note he'd written on his desk, "Uh, *Billy*, just drop in any time. I'm always here, available for a friendly man to man chat, as it were. I want you to think of me as a friend." He smiled broadly. Billy thought he was just pausing but soon realized he was all finished.

"Thank you, sir, thank you very much."

"Please," Mr. Hughes said, gesturing again like a cop halting traffic, "let's not be so formal, *Bill*. After all, we're going to be friends, right?" Billy noddd. "Sure."

"So, why don't we just forget this 'sir' business and call me Mr. Hughes."

Billy wanted to go and get out of there. He was tired and weak with hunger and the still, stale air of the room seemed to be suffocating him.

"Okay, *Mr. Hughes*. Thanks a lot. I'll remember if I have any problems."

"Sure. Fine." Mr. Hughes waved him off. Billy got up and left.

It was just getting dark outside when Billy came out. He stood for just a moment under the portals of the building. He was weak and shaky from not having eaten all day, perspiring, a little light-headed. He breathed deeply of the cool autumn air.

The rush hour was just beginning now and the traffic on the wide, one-way street that ran past the far end of the schoolyard was becoming heavy. The traffic moved along at a slow pace, though not bumper to bumper, except when backed up behind a stop light and the sounds of the motors running and the exhaust pipes and the occasional honking of horns made a fast, soft, rhythmic sound.

In front of the school was a small tree, cottonwood, he thought, though he wasn't sure that that was what it was. He'd missed it that morning when the fog was so dense.

The tree was growing on a small patch of

ground where a little green lawn, too, had been planted. The tree was not a young tree. He could tell by its shape, the thickness of the trunk and the texture of the bark that it was not a young tree. It should have been much larger, he thought. It would have been larger had it had more space to grow and probably the school building blocked out the sun most of the time.

The roots of the tree grew up under the sidewalk causing the concrete to rise and swell. It cracked jaggedly. There were sparse grass and scrawny little twigs growing up from the dirt through the crack in the cement.

He walked down the steps and under the tree and shuffled back and forth on the ground there through the leaves that had fallen and felt them crackle under his feet.

CHAPTER VIII

The next morning he went first to the office and registered for the classes he would take. Afterward, he was told, Mr. Hughes wanted to see him.

The door to Mr. Hughes's office was open and as soon as Billy walked into the outer office he could see him sitting behind his desk, his hands neatly folded in front of him talking to someone out of Billy's line of vision. Mr. Hughes looked up and saw him and smiled and motioned with one hand. "Come on in," he said.

The other person in Mr. Hughes's office was a big, powerfully built black boy. He was dressed the Afro way and his hair was a modified natural. His thick lips were unsmiling as he looked Billy up and down through narrowed eyes.

"Have a seat, Billy," Mr. Hughes told him. He sat.

"Now, then. I forgot to mention one thing during our little talk yesterday afternoon. You see, we have a new program here at Lincoln. It's called the Big Brother—or Big Sister, if applicable—Program and it is designed to help the new student get his, ah, school legs, as it were, if you know what I mean." Mr. Hughes chuckled. "All entering seventh-grade students have a Big Brother and so do transfer students. We think it's a good idea. Won't make you feel so all alone in a strange environment." The black boy was sitting with his big body casually draped in and over the chair. He didn't look attentive in the least; he looked the way Billy felt but was trying to hide: bored by Mr. Hughes and wishing he'd quit. He had his head tilted back and was watching Billy and Mr. Hughes at a down-his-nose angle.

"Billy White Hawk, I want you to meet *your* Big Brother, Curtiss Brown. Curtiss, Billy White Hawk."

The two boys mumbled hellos.

"Curtiss will show you the ropes, help you get acquainted and make a few friends. Have you made out your class schedule yet? Of course you have. May I see it? Thank you. Oh, fine, fine. Art, phys. ed., history, music, algebra, study hall. Curtiss take a look. Do you have any of these same classes?" He held out Billy's class schedule for Curtiss to see and Curtiss leaned over in his chair and glanced at the card. "Yeah," he said. "Three."

"Oh fine. Lovely. You can take him to class with you." He looked at the clock on his wall. "My, you boys had better run along or you'll be late!"

Curtiss had what Billy later came to know as a typical "cool" walk, struttin' his stuff, pimpin' along, a rhythmic saunter. Together they walked out of Mr. Hughes's office and down the deserted hall, Curtiss in his cool way in his highly polished black shoes with the metal tips on the heels and Billy in his long, awkward strides in his worn, cracked boots that fit him too snugly.

"Where are we going, Curtiss?" he asked when they'd gone almost the length of the hall.

"Fo'get that *Curtiss* shee-it, man. The name's Ibutu. Dig? Ibutu." Billy nodded. Curtiss shook his head contemptuously.

"Hey man, what town you from?"

"I'm from a place in Idaho. Not a town. Just a place."

"A place, huh? What you mean 'a place but not a town.' You talkin' crazy, boy."

"I mean, it's . . . well, do you know what a reservation is?"

"You mean where they keep them Injuns? Fahhh out! You mean you a Injun? That is too much." He slapped his hands together and whirled around. "Ooooo eeeeeeee! A Injun. Hee hee hee." He became suddenly sober.

"First, Injun boy, we ah going to our art class. Okay. That's where we belong this hour. Look on your card." Billy wished Lincoln didn't have a Big Brother Program and that it didn't include him.

"Then," Ibutu added, "I'm cuttin' you loose. You can find your own way around okay, now, can't you? Good."

There was a glass display case in the wall just outside the art room. It had a few ceramic pottery

91

pieces on display. Crude, they were hand-built, lopsided, childish pieces in loud, shiny glazes. The sign said EIGHTH-GRADE POTTERY.

The art teacher was a fragile-looking man, short and slightly built. A fluttering, birdlike creature, not yet middle-aged. He was busy with a charcoal drawing when Ibutu and Billy came in. He didn't even look up. Billy went over to him and still the fragile-looking man kept busy with his drawing. He stepped back and looked at it, studied, pondered, then moved in close and took another stroke. Billy was standing behind him watching, fascinated. The man was forming a small-town street scene. He was good. His drawing had a good feel to it, a feel of a quiet small town of long ago. Shadows. Lots of shadows. When the clean-up buzzer sounded the man put the charcoal down. He looked at his drawing and shook his head.

"Excuse me, sir," Billy said. The man turned, surprised. He smiled at Billy. His eyes were soft blue and they had crinkly lines around the edges. He had a sparse mustache. "Yes, what can I do for you?"

"I'm supposed to be in this class. My name is Billy White Hawk." The man held out his hand. "Glad to know you, Billy. I'm Mr. Barrows," he said. His handshake was firm even though his hands were small and soft.

"Listen, I'd like to show you around and explain what general direction I want the class to move in and tell you about the plans but there isn't time for all that now. Here, let me sign your class schedule. And let me see ... where'd be the best place ... you can sit over there at table three, okay? See you tomorrow." And then the bell rang signaling that it was time to go to the next class.

The history teacher was like a twin of Mr.

Hughes only more unsure of himself and afraid: he didn't have the safety of a private office. All he had was a big, cold, classroom full of inattentive, disrespectful students.

The English teacher insulted everyone, calling them "You people," or "You people such as you are." and whenever he accidentally said something which he considered beyond the group's understanding he'd say, "but I forget who I'm talking to, don't I?"

In phys. ed. Billy had to spend the hour walking up and down the bleachers in the gym because he didn't have a gym suit and Mr. King never let anybody just sit there, gym suit or no gym suit.

Study hall had an old lady overseer. She sat half-reading a book, half-watching the class. She sat at the back of the room behind the row of desks.

There was noon dancing in the gym by a jukebox on wheels they brought and plugged into the wall, turning the volume up full blast. Billy sat in the bleachers watching. He caught sight of Ibutu dancing with a pretty black girl. He watched and listened, mesmerized.

The soul music poured loudly out of the jukebox and shook the whole gymnasium. The dancers moved in perfect time, turning, clapping, shaking their heads and shoulders and hips, undulating. Their steps were intricate, complicated, practiced like exhibition dancing. Billy'd never seen anything like it.

"Ooooo eeeeee!" Billy heard a girl near him squeal. She was a little, skinny girl about twelve years old. "Look at Richard," she said breathlessly to another girl beside her. "Yeah, girl. Richard cool! He bad."

For forty-five minutes the dancing continued, wild and soulful, bad and boss and black. Noon dancing. Frantic. He wondered if it happened daily. They must do it a lot.

It was almost a tribal sort of dancing, he thought. He remembered seeing the tribal dances of other nearby tribes (his own tribe had long since forgotten theirs) when he'd gone to Wellpinit, Toppenish, Nespelem. In the summertime celebrations were held in these places, gambling and drinking and dancing. Perhaps most importantly dancing. The old chiefs would turn out in all their splendor, the war bonnets of many eagle feathers that almost touched the ground and their dance was slow and dignified. The young men war dancers were bare-bodied except for loincloths and they wore tail feathers and porcupine quill headdresses and bells hung around their ankles and their faces were painted. They danced like this too, like this strange Kweauss tribe ... frantically, fast, with a kind of fury, the way, a long time ago, a warrior prepared for battle. And the dances that everyone did, the men and women and children, holding hands and moving around the circle while the drums beat and the voices rang out. It made them feel all together, part of one whole.

Down on the gym floor he could see Ibutu dancing. The sweat stood out in beads on his forehead and was running down his face. His body moved smoothly, under control, graceful. Powerful. "I heard it on the grapevine," the music said, the tribal music. "Oooooo eeeeee!" the skinny little seventh grader squealed shrilly.

When Billy got home that evening there was a note from Alice Fay that said she had to work overtime at the office but she'd put his dinner in the oven.

He looked in the oven. "Dinner" was a pie tin of thawed-out fishsticks. Alice Fay had probably intended they should keep warm but she'd left the heat on too high and the fishsticks were all dried out now and blackened.

He took them into the living room and switched on the TV.

A movie was on, a beach party movie with cute teen-age girls in bikinis strutting around a beach. Feckless rock and roll music played in the background. Someone shouted, "Surf's up" and everyone ran out carrying their surfboards. Then it showed them riding the big waves back, a girl on a boy's shoulders, her arms extended, the wind in her hair. Everyone was smiling. Everyone was having a good time.

Billy lifted his legs over the arm of a big, comfortable chair and settled back to eat his fishsticks and watch the beach party.

CHAPTER IX

It was December now and cold and raining all the time. Billy was failing algebra, though this was not noticed except when the report cards came out and the F was found written upon it. He'd made no friends; there was no one for him to be with and talk to.

If Tom were alive ... he'd often think, well he would do this or that ... we could go here or there. What would Tom do if he could come to Lincoln and see what it was like, how isolated

Billy was there, how Curtiss Brown alias Ibutu and the others made a joke of him. Curtiss Brown ... Hah! Why they'd get that bastard. They'd get him good, Tom and Billy. And when they were all done and he'd paid his dues for all the insult and humiliation he'd caused, he'd *never* mess with anybody like that again ... after he got himself picked up and put back together.

It was worse, much worse than school at Bradley. Worse because of the vast strangeness of the place, worse because apart from the school itself there was no place he belonged.

He said to himself, even if he could, still there was nothing about them he'd care to be a part of, them in their woolly buffalo hair and their proud blackness and their loud boisterous laughter and strange, mindblowing talk. Yet he watched them being together, he envied them their bonds, the common thing they all knew and were that let them understand and be like each other.

There was one person who wasn't a part of them, though, and wanted to be. Little Bernie Leiborwitz, who was a white boy, and he didn't seem to know how he would ever make it "in" with Curtiss Brown and Haskell and Willie Joe and Jay El and the rest.

Bernie wasn't like other people, *no other people.* There was something going on a different way inside his head, a strange, unusual something that made him see things the way he wanted. He wasn't stupid, no that wasn't it. He always got A's in algebra and mostly in his other classes too, and he could ask relevant questions in class.

Bernie had lots of hair, dull, dark blond-gray hair that was thick and matted and dirty-looking all the time. He never tied his shoes, either. He didn't take the laces out. The laces were always there, hanging loose and dangling. His eyes were deep-set, dark in their sockets, always open wide and round and staring, staring. It was hard to tell just what color Bernie's eyes were, they were always changing, it seemed, sometimes grayish sometimes a shade of green, sometimes brown. Billy had three classes with Bernie, algebra, and phys. ed. and music appreciation.

In both algebra and health, sometime during the study periods after the lessons were done Bernie would ask to tell one of his "original jokes." Usually the teacher would say, "Sorry, not today, maybe some other time," and the class would say, "AAWWWWWWW. C'mon. Let Bernie tell us an original joke. Yeah, man, he good. Bernie tell good jokes. Heee heee hee." And usually the teacher would smile and shake his head.

There were a few times, though, when the teachers would agree and Bernie told jokes to the class. They would sit at their desks while Bernie walked up to the front of the room and while he stood before them, his eyes closed, thinking of what he was going to say, they would grin and roll their eyes at one another. The teacher, too, would grin with the class while they all waited.

Bernie's jokes were never funny. Never. And there was no one in the whole school who believed that Bernie's jokes were funny, yet when he told a joke everyone would throw their heads back and slap their thighs and open their mouths wide and laugh, rocking back and forth and they would applaud and Bernie would stand before his audience, a little smile on his crazy little face, just so pleased with himself and he would take short bows down from his waist and say, "Thank you. Thank you. Thank you very much, ladies and gentlemen. You're too kind." And this would start a fresh round of laughter. "You good, Burn-nard! You a good comedian. Fah out, man. Bad. Groovy."

Bernie's jokes were always about scientists, because, he said, he himself would one day be a great scientist so he was most interested in science and anything having to do with it. The jokes were almost all alike, variations of the eccentric scientist putting down laymen.

"There was this scientist and he took his lady friend out for a night on the town. They went to a fancy-pants nightclub with a band and champagne and a pretty lady singer with a sparkly dress down to here sitting on the piano. The works. Now, the scientist, being a scientist, had his head full of very important matters and he had forgotten to dress up and was still wearing his bathrobe, which he'd put on after he'd taken a shower at home. The snooty man at the door who pretended he was French, told the scientist he couldn't come in unless he wore a tuxedo. He was quite a mundane character, as you can see. When the scientist wouldn't move, but just stood there, the fake Frenchman got angry and his face turned red and he yelled, 'Get out of here, monsieur, this instant, before I call the police and have you hauled away in a black maria.' The scientist looked the snooty old guy right in the eye and said in a very calm and dignified manner, 'I ain't goin' anywhere, Jack, until you get off my foot.'"

Like young Bernie Leiborwitz, Billy, too, had become a comical figure.

It had begun almost right away, since that first day when Curtiss Brown-Ibutu, found out he was a Injun from a resahvashun. At first it may have been only good-natured kidding, 'cept for the grin and the way Curtiss rolled his eyes around to the other boys when he made WOO WOO WOO war

98

whoops when Billy came walking down the hall. He'd ask him questions in front of his gang, Jay El and Haskell and the others in the same manner of speaking that people at Lincoln used when addressing Bernie, as if he could not see the offensiveness. "Didya live in one of them te-pees. Didya weave baskets? How come they let you off the resahvation? You better look out, boy. I heard they's fittin' to send all the Injuns back again. Better lay off the fire water awhile, huh?"

Then there was Elmira Hodges. She was Suyappi, with a face and body shaped like a potato and pale skin dotted with infected pimples. She always wore long, fancy, dangling earrings. Haskell and Ibutu kept coming up to Billy, in the phys. ed. locker room, or cornering him in the hall, and telling him how they knew "a chick, man, a ril fox and she dig you, by the name of Elmira. She hot for your bod, man. No lie. Billy think we puttin' him on. We ain't puttin' him on. Hey, Willie Joe, tell the man ain't it the truth that Elmira Hodges say she dig Billy?" "Shee-it, yeah, that the truth." He never answered them when they told him of Elmira's admiration. They wouldn't stop.

One day he saw Haskell and Curtiss talking with Elmira in the hallway. He was at his locker putting books away. He could hear them say, "No lie, Elmira. He just too shy to speak up for hisself. Go on up to him. Just go ax him."

He'd just slammed closed the locker door when Elmira came walking up to him. She was smiling. She had crooked, yellowed teeth.

"Hi," she said, "nice day, isn't it." He nodded. "I'm Elmira." He nodded again, pensive. "I hear ... I mean, look, let's not play games. I got your message." She blushed. "I'd be honored to go to the dance with you Saturday." Her eyes were shining as she stood looking up at him, clutching her books close to her bosom. He could hear Haskell and Ibutu giving each other some skin (some hand slaps) and laughing.

"Look, Elmira. I gotta go, see you around," Billy said, running away.

Then one day the facade of good-naturedness came to an end and the fooling around became up-front malicious.

In phys. ed. class Billy usually stayed out of the way of the others as best he could. They were playin some kind of game and they wanted to win, he'd let them, give them the ball, miss his turn, anything to avoid their wrath. This particular afternoon, though, he didn't do that. They were playing basketball. Haskell wanted the ball. Ordinarily Billy would have let him have it, would have almost handed it to him. Haskell was like a snowplow and kept coming at Billy, going after that ball. This time, though, Billy wouldn't let go for anything. He knew he should. He knew it was stupid. I'm just axin' for it, he said to himself, hanging on. Haskell was furious. Maybe it would be like in the movies and they would gain new respect for him because he wouldn't let them push him around, he thought. Haskell knocked Billy down accidently while trying to get the ball away from him. The gym teacher blew the whistle.

"Motha!" Haskell spat and let him have it with his big black fist.

"I didn't do nothin'," Haskell said when the gym teacher got there. Billy's nose was bleeding all over his shirt and all over the floor. He was still holding the ball.

"Didn't you hear me blow the whistle, White Hawk?" Mr. King asked.

"Yeah," he said. He was holding his T-shirt to his nose, trying to stop the bleeding.

"I didn't do nothin'," Haskell repeated, "I didn't do nothin'. This boy here, he fell down." The buzzer sounded for shower time and Billy got up and walked off the floor.

It was after the incident in phys. ed. Billy noticed how he'd be walking along the hall and when he got near a group of boys standing together talking they'd fall suddenly quiet and they'd watch him pass, sometimes glaring, sometimes grinning. Then after he passed he'd hear them break into laughter. Once he turned and looked back and found Jay El following close behind, mocking his long strides, the way he walked with his heels run over and his arms swinging loosely at his sides.

His sleep for a long time had been empty of dreams. Then he knew there were dreams that came, dreams he awoke from feeling afraid, but he couldn't remember them.

Through all of this there was something for him, though, something new and good he'd discovered and this was painting.

He did painting of the Benewah countryside in the summer, casein on pieces of cardboard, and Mr. Barrows admired them and said, "Oh, these are fine, Billy, just fine." And he did a charcoal drawing of Joe sitting partly in shadows on the front steps of the cabin. He'd never thought he was much good at such things. He wasn't a good draftsman. His drawings weren't realistic, they didn't show things as they really looked, as a photograph would. Mr. Barrows told him it didn't matter so much, that part of it, and he taught him composition and perspective, texture, techniques and how to mix colors. It was the feeling, he told Billy, the feeling that mattered. Transfer your feelings about

101

the subject onto your canvas, communicate these feelings. "Sensitive lines," Mr. Barrows said, "well handled."

Billy liked painting. He liked working, making something of his own. He liked watching Mr. Barrows work too. Sometimes he'd get a pass from study hall to come into the art room and work.

He did a painting of colors, autumn colors, yellow, red, orange, brown, overlapping with bold black lines separating, connecting. "Marvelous!" Mr. Barrows said when he saw it. "Just marvelous." And when he went away Ibutu came over to Billy's easel. "I just want to see what's so mahvelous as all that," he said. He looked at the painting and went away again.

When Billy got to school and the next day he found the painting of autumn colors and a small one of the sunset through dense branches in the display case and a little sign that said these were the paintings of Billy White Hawk, grade nine. Some students were gathered around looking at the paintings. In spite of all the trouble Billy felt happy, proud of his paintings, proud that he could do paintings.

"Mistah Bay-rows and him must got somethin' goin'. Yeah. The little faggot see that pitcha and he say, 'Oh, mahvelous.' " It was Ibutu's voice.

He began to see things in terms of paintings. He noticed how shadows fell, the quality of light, the colors and textures. He longed for his own paints and brushes and canvases, instead of pieces of cardboard, his own working space.

Alice Fay was gone out a lot these days. It used to be she'd say she had to work overtime, then come home in the small hours of the morning. Lately she'd quit saying why she was late and two or three times she'd even spent the night out.

Billy watched television and thought of ideas for new paintings. There was going to be an intercity junior and senior high school art exhibit in the spring. He dreamed of his work on display there, of a whole wall hung with his work and the thousands of strangers that would go to that exhibit and stop to look and comment on his paintings.

It was cold in the apartment. The superintendent turned the radiator heat off early, around nine or ten o'clock. Once Mrs. Quinch's daughter, Annie, was missing. Mrs. Quinch knocked at the door and when Billy answered, pushed her way inside and searched the apartment for her daughter, the closets, the shower stall, behind the davenport and under Alice Fay's bed, all the time muttering, "Where you got her hid? I know she's here somewhere. I can feel her vibes." When she finally found little Annie, crouched on the fire escape outside Billy's windows, she dragged her off by the hair slapping her. Then pushing the crying girl out of the apartment she shouted back over her shoulder at Billy, "My girl is a minor, you know. Why you molester. I'll call the cops on you. Have you hauled off to jail where you rightfully belong!" He'd heard no more of it but felt a little nervous, though, for quite a few days afterward. Every time a police car would stop out front because of some disturbance at Arnie's Hideaway, Billy would fear they were coming after him.

A few days before Christmas vacation Mr. Barrows asked Billy how he'd like to be in the citywide art exhibit in May. "There's a nice prize, fifty dollars. I think you're good. I think you have a good chance of winning, Billy," he said. And Billy begin to daydream of the exhibit, and beyond, when he was older and a world-renowned painter and *Life* magazine devoted an entire issue to him on his twenty-fifth birthday.

Joe sent him a card in mid-December. It was a giant card and it had a huge, jolly Santa Claus face on the front with a pasted-on fluffy white cotton beard. It said: "To a wonderful son on Christmas Day. May all year long be happy and gay." Inside Joe signed his name formally, Joseph William White Hawk, Sr., and in parenthesis, "(Your Dad)." That was all, no note.

On Christmas Day Billy and Alice Fay went to a cafeteria downtown where they were having a special turkey dinner, all you can eat for one dollar and seventy-five cents per person. It was all gaily decorated with pine boughs and big red bows and fake foam-snow and they were playing, "White Christmas" and songs like that over their loud speaker systems. The other customers were mostly old people, all dressed up and eating alone. There was one very young mother with a boy of two years there too. The young mother was having trouble making the boy stay seated and eat. Billy thought she couldn't have been more than eighteen or nineteen. Billy and Alice Fay both ate heartily. Alice Fay had seconds, Billy had thirds. Then they went to a movie where a Hollywood muscle man played Jesus.

When they got home Mrs. Mobley from upstairs invited them to come up and visit awhile. She had eggnog laced liberally with brandy, the way, she said, her late husband liked it, though she herself never cared much for the stuff. She just was in the habit now, she said, of making some at Christmas. Mrs. Mobley played her electric organ and sang and asked them to join in and they did. Alice Fay's voice was almost as bad as Mrs. Mobley's, Billy noticed, and he knew his own singing was nothing to brag about. It was fun. They san "Hark! the Herald Angels Sing" and "O Little Town of Bethlehem." Billy was getting a nice, warm glow from the liberally laced eggnog. They were singing "God Rest Ye Merry, Gentlemen" when Mrs. Quinch upstairs began thumping on the ceiling and yelling in her wretched, thin voice, "Quiet down there. Quiet I say, you damn rounders. I'll have you all locked up!" And that was the end of the party at Mrs. Mobley's. Mrs. Mobley gave Billy a book of illustrated Bible stories and Alice Fay a little white prayer book with her name engraved in gold letters. They thanked her and wished they'd had a present for her and she told them the party was present enough for her.

At home they watched TV for a time, then Alice Fay said she was very tired and went to bed.

He went to sleep on his davenport bed.

When he woke up again he knew he'd been dreaming because his hand was extended, as if he were reaching out for something, yet he could remember nothing. He heard loud talking and laughing and horn blowing coming from the street below. He got up on his knees on the davenport and lifted the shade.

It was just after 2:00 A.M. and Arnie had kicked out the Christmas merrymakers. There was an old, blond woman down there standing away from the rest with a man. They were both very drunk, swaying as they clung to each other. They were kissing. The hideaway crowd gathered around them and applauded and cheered and blew their noisemakers. The couple was still kissing when Billy dropped the shade and lay back down. Just think, he thought, I'm going to be in a big exhibit. Me. I might win a prize. Fah out!

105

CHAPTER X

The painting was of the old men singers he remembered seeing at the celebrations. They were sitting in a circle around a big rawhide drum and their faces were lined, their mouths open, singing. They held drumsticks in their hands and were beating upon the drum. It was a night scene, the singer's faces illuminated by firelight.

"Fabulous," Mr. Barrows said. It was done in oils on a canvas board. Mr. Barrows and Billy matted it. Mr. Barrows said words like, "Subtle," "Effective, captures the feeling." "Nice." "This one," Mr. Barrows said, "oh, definitely, this one will go to the spring exhibit. You must get to work and do more now."

When school was out Billy found Haskell and Jay El, Ibutu and Willie Joe standing around outside the building. When Ibutu saw Billy he flicked his cigarette down and stepped on it. He came walking toward him.

"Hey, Injun," Ibutu drawled, stepping in Billy's way. Billy was afraid. He knew he could fight all right. He wasn't bad. He knew how to handle himself. Yet, it had been a long time and he knew Curtiss Brown was fast and powerful, though he'd never seen him in a fight. He was probably good and there were all his friends there standing around watching and waiting. He was looking at

Billy squinty-eyed, with his head tilted back and to one side.

"Hey, Redskin," he said, "tell me all about yourself, boy, I mean us being Big Brotha and little brotha and all, we should get better acquainted." He turned his head slightly, glancing at his friends and smiled. "Show me how you can rain dance, okay? I always wondered how you did it. C'mon, do a little dance. It would be lots of fun. Educational."

"Look, Curtiss, or Ibutu or whoever you are, I'm in a hurry now." Billy tried to step around him but it didn't work. Curtiss grabbed him with both fists by the collar of his jacket. "Not so fast, motha," he snarled. Without realizing he was going to do it, his fist shot out punching Curtiss' nose. Curtiss shook his head back and forth hard, not letting go of Billy. He narrowed his eyes, looked at him increduously, "You crazy, motha," he said and, still holding him with one hand, he swung back his other, powerful fist and came up alongside Billy's head. He hit him in the eye. Again and again he hit him. Billy struggled to free himself from Curtiss' hold and tried to escape the blows but it did no good.

Inside his head it felt like his brains had been jarred loose and scrambled up. He started blacking out and Curtiss let go of him and let him fall to the pavement. The last thing he heard was Mr. Hughes's voice saying, "Okay, boys, now that's enough. Haskell, stay back. That's enough, I say."

When Billy came to he was lying on a cot in the infirmary and Mr. Hughes was standing over him, a cigar stub hanging out of the corner of his mouth. Billy tried to sit up but his head hurt so badly he lay back down again. He could feel the swelling on his face, the skin pulling tight.

"This is bad, very bad for your record young man. Fighting never got anybody anywhere."

"But I was only ..."

"Now, tut tut ... not another word. Did you or did you not hit Curtiss Brown first?"

"Yeah, I did, I guess. Sure."

"We don't approve of violence here at Lincoln. We believe if two parties have a disagreement there are better ways of settling it. Why, you could've come to me. I could've acted as mediator. This will look terrible on your record young man. Nobody likes a troublemaker. Listen, boy, if you're having a hard time adjusting here why don't you just come right out and say so. Come into my office and talk things over. It helps to talk things over. I'm a counselor, you know. I know you come from a much different background than most of the others. Don't think I don't realize the going must get rough. Come and talk to me. We'll work on it together. You must try harder. Try to adjust. Okay?"

"Yeah, okay, Mr. Hughes."

Mr. Hughes called Alice Fay on the phone and told her that Billy had attacked another boy with no apparent provocation; that the school was putting him on six weeks' probation during which time his activities would be watched very carefully.

"Mr. Hughes sounds like a pretty nice guy, Billy," Alice Fay said, "like he's concerned about you, you know. He wants to help. He says you're having an unusual amount of difficulty adjusting, it seems. He says he's on your side, he said for me to tell you that, tell him I'm on his side as I'm on all my boys' side, he said. But he can't do it alone and he doesn't think you're trying very hard." Alice Fay was sitting with a glass of sherry in her hand, her hair done up in brush rollers, watching TV.

By the time the bottle of sherry was emptied

and the late news was over, Alice Fay was more than ready for bed.

"Listen, Billy," she said, thickly, "I warned you now, didn't I, about not giving me any trouble. Lord knows I got troubles of my own. *Oh, have I got troubles.* If you don't do better ... I mean if they actually *expel* you, well, I just can't have you around any more." She waved her hand in a gesture of dismissal. She staggered unsurely over to his chair. "Do you understand?" she asked, leaning down.

"Yeah. I understand."

"Good," she said. "Now"—she punched him lightly on the shoulder—"let's see you get in there and adjust, goddamit!" She giggled and went off to bed.

Billy stayed up late watching Humphrey Bogart doing the man's man bit. He wondered what Alice Fay's troubles were. It had to do with the staying out. It could be a man, or drinking or men and drinking. Maybe Alice Fay in her loneliness had turned to drinking in taverns (Alice Fay, a common bar fly?) ... something she'd always despised as "throwing oneself around" like a "dirty, low-down reservation Indian" and if she were "throwing herself around" this way, then it must be hurting her. Or maybe it was something much different. He didn't have any idea, really. He wondered if they might really expel him. He had ideas for new paintings: impressions of a forest, in green and yellow and black. Adjust. Adjust, the man said, you could if you really tried. Hah. Did it ever occur to him that Billy might not want to adjust? "Here's looking at you, Kid," Humphrey said to Lauren. He really knew how to treat a woman. Then some interference from a low-flying plane or an electrical appliance in another apartment and the picture started flopping over. Adjust, he thought. He was a boy, not a TV set. He would ask Mr. Barrows for a note to give to his study hall teacher so he might be allowed to go to the art room to paint.

All that week there was talk of the Friday talent show in Billy's music appreciation class. The teacher, a tiny black woman by the name of Miss Lewis, wanted everyone to have an act prepared. "Even if it's just playing some simple little tune on the bells," she said. "Whoever doesn't will automatically get an F grade for the week."

The big day came and it wasn't a bad show. There were tap dancers, bespangled baton twirlers and several very good vocal groups. Some were not good: an accordion player's rendition of "Tuna Fish," and taps played on the xylophone.

When everyone had had their turn and the time was almost up, Miss Lewis told them how they'd done a good job and she hoped a good time was had by all. There were still fifteen minutes left before the dismissal bell. Someone in the back piped up, "Why don't Bernie tell a joke?" And right away other voices joined in. "Yeah. Right on. We want Bernie. We want a joke."

Bernie's act had been a disappointment. He'd read a short poem about death no one had enjoyed. Now, he was smiling broadly when he came walking up to the little crude platform where the microphone was set up. Everyone was laughing and stamping their feet and clapping their hands. He put up his hands signaling them to quiet. When they'd quieted down he began:

"Well, once there was a scientist," he started. A girl giggled, then clamped her hand over her mouth. "And this scientist was talking to a man who was trying to perturb the scientist. It was too much. The man was saying, 'Your church is just dumb, you namby-pamby. Only a moron would take such a dumb church seriously.' The scientist just smiled. 'And your wife . . . is she ugly! Ooooooeeeee! Where'd you find her, in your neighbor's garbage can?' The scientist said, 'You're quite right, my good fellow. She is rather unattractive, isn't she?' The man said, 'And those kids of yours. Man, they are something else. When you take them out for a walk, you got to obey the leash law.' The scientist, very cool, just chuckled, 'Now that you mention it, I do.' Then the man said, 'And how about science? What a drag. Talk about insignificant? Skinnie Minnie! Science is nothing but a farce, a discipline for fools, without meaning, without use. Science, the great waste of time.' Now this last remark angered the scientist, as well it might, ladies and gentlemen, as well it might. 'My good man,' he said, trying to be civilized, 'You are too ignorant to realize what you're saying and therefore may be forgiven. You may insult me, my religion, my wife and children, all you care to, it doesn't matter. When you insult science, well, then you're going too far!' The man answered, 'And you, sir, you are a bubblehead.' 'That's better,' the scientist said and walked away."

The class applauded and roared with laughter. "Too much, Bur-nard." "Bad." "That was a boss joke." "We kin dig it."

When the laughter had died down and Bernie had taken his final bows and stepped down a voice was heard to say, "And how about Billy? Billy, man, cantcho do nothin'?" Jay El. Billy looked to Miss Lewis. She was small like a wren with little twigs for legs and arms, a small round head, short fuzzy hair. She was grinning in that same mocking way just like the others. Clearly Miss Lewis wouldn't tell her charges to cool it.

"Aw, c'mon, Billy, don't be like that. Why you so stubborn, boy? Do a war dance for us, yeah." "Sing a Injun song for us." "Using some cool ones. We wanta hear some soul music, redskin style. Do it." Billy crouched as low down as he could behind his desk.

"Oh, he just bashful. He know lotsa good jokes. C'mon, boy, don't be so cold. Here we is *starvin'* for some jokes." He wished the floor would open up and swallow him. "Heee heee heee." They began stomping their feet and whistling and clapping their hands like they did for Bernie. He heard someone make that war whoop sound, then another and another. "Wooo wooo wooo." "We want Billy. Yeah, we want the chief. Go ahead, chief. Go ahead, Geronimo!"

Very angry, he walked to the platform. He didn't know what he was going to say.

He stood before them, clutching the microphone stem with one hand. A sea of black, brown, tan faces, smiling, mocking faces and a few Suyappi scattered throughout. Bernie was not smiling, though, strangely. Maybe he thought that Billy would replace him, Billy thought.

Some girls in the front row were grinning, some with their hands over their mouths, and rolling their eyes, poking each other in the ribs with their elbows.

"What you going to do, Billy?" one of the girls called out. "You going to tell us a Indyun joke?" and her remark was followed by low laughter.

His knees felt weak. His hands were shaking.

"Yeah." He nodded. "Sure, if that's what you want, I'll tell you a joke."

"How about a rain dance," somebody called. "Imitate Sitting Bull," someone else called.

"Maybe after I finish the joke," he told them.

He began slowly, his eyes sweeping over his audience. He was smiling. "I think you're going to like this one, folks," he said. "Right on, chief," someone shouted.

"Well, this is the way it was: once there was a big country. Many tribes lived in this country. Sometimes they had fights and disagreements but they always managed to work it out, okay. These people were light brown.

"One day a ship or two came from somewhere over the ocean with some funny-looking, white-skinned people. White, like the underbellies of frogs, the people thought, and very up-tight besides. The whites were running away from home because they weren't being treated right back there. The brown people took pity on them. They said, 'Look, they need help, the poor things. Let's have them stay with us. We got plenty of room.' And so they did.

"It wasn't long, though, until the white-skinned people had become a great many and each day more and more were coming in ships from across the sea. It got so the white-skinned people forgot how the land belonged to the brown-skinned people. They had short memories. They even forgot how the browns had given them food and showed them how to grow crops and helped them survive. They thought the land belonged to them, that they had 'discovered' it. They had guns and cannons and things like that. They plotted land and built fences and made boundaries and drove the brown-skinned people away. They liked to call them 'savages' and they liked to kill them. They wanted *all* the land for themselves.

"'No matter,'" the brown ones said, 'there's plenty of land further West. Come on, let's go,' and they packed up and moved.

113

"The frog bellies captured some brown people and tried to make slaves out of them but it didn't work, for the brown-skinned people were slaves to no man. The frog bellies shrugged and said, 'They are hopeless. So lazy they'd rather be beaten and starved and shot than work. Now that's lazy!'

"Then the frog bellies brought over a bunch of black skins to be their slaves. The black ones didn't have so much pride and they worked out okay.

"After many years the black ones were given their freedom and were no longer slaves but as it turned out, as free men they were just as bad, if not worse, than their white captors. The brown people, meanwhile, had formed an intertribal coalition and were holding secret meetings to decide what must be done.

'We made a grave mistake,' one old man told the people, 'we shouldn't have helped those first renegades. Then they would've died off the first winter and no more would've followed.'

"A young man said, 'It is of no use, old man, saying what we should've done way back then. What does it matter? What are we to do now with all these uppity blacks and uppity whites?' There were many suggestions made, from making slaves of them to shipping them to either segregated or integrated concentration camps. Finally it was decided.

"On a certain day several months later the uppity blacks and uppity whites were taken by surprise and pushed all the way across the continent and pushed right into the Atlantic Ocean. When the last one was pushed in and went down for the last time, I don't know if the last one was black or white, the brown people cheered. The President said, 'It's too bad, the way it had to end, but doggone it, they just couldn't learn how to act right.' And so, rid of the blacks and whites, the country

114

went back to being much like it was before, open and wild, quiet. Nobody was ever going to be let in again because they couldn't cut it at home."

Billy felt weak and drained of energy. He looked out over his audience. Why didn't they react? They were sitting quietly, looking at him. Leaving his books at his seat, he stepped down off the platform and walked out the door.

CHAPTER XI

Billy called Alice Fay at work and told her he'd be going to a movie that night, that he was going with some school friends and they were going to treat and he'd be home by midnight or before. It was Friday night and he knew she probably wouldn't even be there but he didn't want to take any chances. She said all right. Have a good time. He had a lot of thinking to do. He'd done an awful thing that day. An awful, unforgivable, no-way-of-justifying sort of thing he would have to try to figure a way to get out of.

He walked down near the edge of the bay where the logs came floating in. He went on a dock and looked into the murky green water and saw fishes swimming. He wondered how they could live in shallow water like that so close to the city, so close to where ships docked. He walked on then, along the street that ran next to the water; there was very little traffic there. It was once supposed to

have been, in the good old days, after the pioneers
settled and the town was going good and the
people all came looking for free land and the port
was going full blast, a tough place down there by
the water front. A place where tough seagoing men
and roughnecks and crooks and loose women of all
kinds hung out. He went into a little tavern that
had a big window that looked out into the water.
He wanted a drink, more than a drink. He wanted
to get drunk. He wanted to forget the pain of the
past, the uncertainty of it all, he wanted to forget
Lincoln Junior High School and the awful thing
he'd done that day in music appreciation. He
wanted to forget about poor old Joe and the reservation and how it seemed he was all washed up at
fifteen with no place to go from there. Shee-it, he
thought, then laughed at himself, very amused to
have thought such a word as "shee-it." He had one
dollar and eighty-five cents in his pocket. Alice Fay
gave him this money, at a rate of thirty cents a day
and he was not saving it, it was just that even
when he was hungry he didn't want to go in the
cafeteria and sit among those Kweauss and be either ignored or laughed at. The waitress was a
blond lady he would guess to be about thirty-five
or thereabouts. Her blond hair was obviously dyed,
not obvious only because you could see that down
near her scalp the hair was medium brown for an
inch or so of length but because the color itself was
unnatural. The blond was really white, he saw
when she came close, with a light pink tint. She
had her name embroidered above her left breast on
the white blouse she wore. Dolly, it said. Her hair
was in big petal-curls pinned on top of her head.
Her lipstick was pink, moist, luminescent. Around
her eyes was green cosmetic color and her eyebrows actually non-existent, as if she'd shaved

them off, and in their place were drawn perfect ones, Elizabeth Taylor eyebrows. Altogether, he thought, she was actually quite beautiful. "I want a shot of whiskey," he said when she came to him. She smiled and laid her soft, white hand on his. "Look, honey," she said, "how old are you?" And he mumbled twenty-one. "Don't be in such a hurry to grow up, honey, believe you me it happens soon enough, then you wish you could turn the clock back and get your youth and innocence back again." She looked him in the eyes. Her voice was soft. The false eyelash on one eye was coming loose. He could see the yellow adhesive backing. The eyelashes reminded him of caterpillar legs. "You're listening to the voice of experience, sweetheart," she said, laughing huskily. "There'll be time enough for getting drunk and all this stuff." A group of men at a far table had finished their beers and wanted another round. "Hey, Dolly," one called, "get your beautiful ass over here. Cause you got some thirsty men." "Coming!" she called to them and they laughed and made jokes among themselves of the word she'd used.

"Do you want to be like those guys over there?" she asked Billy. "Just look at them. They ain't got no choice any more. You got your youth and all your life ahead of you. You in school? Good. Stay there. The only way you'll ever get ahead." "Hey, Dolly. Come on, girl, we can't wait all day."

"Okay. Okay," she called to them.

Then, "Go now, boy, get out of here. If you're smart you'll remember what I told you." She patted his hand. He smiled at her. She winked at him with the eye whose lash was coming loose. He was leaving already when she got to the table that'd been calling her. He looked back and saw a man grab her around the waist and pat her on the bottom. Billy went out the door and walked on down away from the docks and buildings to a sandy beach area. It had begun to drizzle. There were no other people except for a young couple and their dog. The man was chasing the woman, and the dog ran close behind jumping up and barking. The man caught the woman, tackling her and making her fall down in the sand with him. He tickled her and she laughed hysterically, breathless, trying to make him stop. He heard her pleading, "Oh, no, don't. Don't. I take it back. I take it back." "What are you, then?" the merciless man demanded, letting up on his tickling a moment, "Tell me." The dog jumped round them wagging his tail. "A kitchen wench!" she laughed, "a kitchen wench." The man quit tickling her and drew her into his arms. "That's much better," he said. She wound her arms around his neck and pressed close to him. The man had a woolly beard and hair that fell to his shoulders. She had hair that fell down past her waist and she wore a sweatshirt and shorts and glass beads about her neck.

They kissed. "Chauvinist pig," she said, and he grabbed her and lifted his hand, wiggling his fingers in gesture of threatening tickles. "Forgive me, master," she said, smiling, and they held each other and kissed. They didn't notice Billy passing by but their dog walked along with him for a while before turning back.

Billy walked down the beach until he was far enough away from them he couldn't hear their voices or make out their features when he looked back. He sat down in the sand and looked at the sea, smelled the salt air. He watched the waves coming in from way far off, a raised cliff of white foam, and breaking on shore. Some sort of birds floated on the waves, nonchalantly, their wings folded under.

The drizzle became heavier and the fog came in. He was getting wet. He didn't care. He looked down the beach and saw the exuberant couple had taken their leave, and their dog. He'd done a thing he would probably be expelled for doing. Then Alice Fay, the bitch, would either send him back or stick him away in reform school. She'd told him all about reform school. She said all she'd have to do is tell the authorities that he was too much to handle, that he was "beyond control," and that would be enough to put him away until he turned eighteen. Just that. Shee-it, he thought. That was the most appropriate word for his collective feelings and thoughts, the most fitting of all words ... simple, direct ... SHEE-IT. He wished the compassionate, pink-haired Dolly was there with him, to hold his hand and tell him all her worldliness had made known to her. He drew a circle in the sand with his finger and a dog in the middle, radial lines emanating from the center dot. Now he had to do something. He couldn't let them just do what they would, just plow him under. He had no chance of speaking for himself, of course, for not only was he just a young kid who didn't know what was going on but he had also hit Haskell first and gotten beaten up and therefore had a very bad mark on his record, which Mr. Hughes pointed out, would follow him the rest of his life. So he needed someone else to stick up for him, someone who had a place in their world, someone who was respected, to talk in his behalf. Surely Alice Fay wouldn't. No, not Alice Fay. If she went she would just agree with everything they told her, then she would pull out one of those dainty handkerchiefs she'd made in BIA school, with the crochet around the border, and the flowers and her initials, A.W., embroidered on it, and dab her eyes and in a whiny voice explain how she'd done the best she could, God knows, to make Billy do like he was supposed to do, but he was already ruined when he came to her, and God knows how it broke her heart to have failed. And Mr. Hughes, and the rest, would comfort her, "There, there, you did enough. Yeah, you mopped and waxed the floors and you spoke out against dirt and drink and you, in defiance of your wretched reservation background, became a machine operator ... think of it, *a machine operator* while your contemporaries remained on the reservation sexing and boozing, messing, doing just what comes naturally, the poor pitiful, weak, naive things. Never in a hundred years could they hope to attain the high pinnacle you've . . . but surely you know all this." "Yes, but Billy, my very own brother ... *my half brother*, really." "There, there, my dear. A person has free will. You couldn't live that boy's life *for* him. After all, there is a limit." Shee-it. Maybe Hughes and Alice Fay would get together over this, discover each other. Go steady. Billy chuckled. Mr. Hughes plus Alice Fay. It would look cute carved in a tree or written on a sidewalk. He was watching the rise and fall, the movement of the waves.

He'd heard people get hooked on the ocean, that once living near it they can't bear to live far away from it. It was a far-out thing, an ocean was. It was fun to watch and think of nothing, to let your thoughts fasten upon nothing and just drift in and out with the waves. He was hooked on the ocean too, in a way. He liked the ocean. He liked watching it. Yet, once seen it wasn't just a physical presence any more. Once you sat and watched, even as he'd done a time ago, the ocean was something you knew was inside you all along. You watched the waves. You thought of the ocean. You *internalized* the ocean. Then you didn't need *it* any more. You knew what it was to you. What was good about coming out here and looking at it again was the salt sea air, the sound of fog horns, the mist. It all had a calming effect. He remembered back home, the crops of grain, golden wheat, pale yellow barley, growing tall and plentiful upon the rolling hills. When summer winds came and shook the steaks you could see the ripples and waves over the hills, an ocean that did not reach as far as this one of water and salt but it was the same, it went on as far as the eye could see, where sky and sea, or sky and earth, met. When he went back and saw the golden oceans of grain he would remember this ocean: the drizzle, the fog, the white caps, the constant movement. He was wet. He was cold. He didn't care. Shee-it! Look at the ocean! Always changing, yet always remaining the same. Old, old, everlasting, always-there ocean. Always changing, shifting, old things coming apart and new things forming, old life dying and new come into being. Always, the waves coming and going. Always changing, still always there, remaining the same. Way in the mist there was a place where waves rose and fell all together and repeated the motion. Staring at that place it looked like it might be a big ocean-going fishing canoe heading out toward the open sea, the steady rise and fall, the white foam in a row like the foam men might make pushing oars through the water and lifting them. He kept watching that thing. An optical illusion, he thought, and nothing more. When darkness fell and he could see no more he got up. He decided he would pay a visit to Mr. Barrows. He could help. Mr. Barrows would know what to do. He walked near the water. The rain had stopped now. The lights of the city reflected off the smooth dark surface of the water. Gently the water rocked and so did the colored city lights. Billy threw a handful of rocks into the water and where he'd thrown them the water broke a moment, the reflection shattering, then quickly recomposed and was as before.

Billy found a public telephone booth and looked up Mr. Barrows' address. It wasn't far away, as it turned out. Mr. Barrows lived in a warehouse loft right on the waterfront. His living area was small, just a stove, frig, single bed and table in one corner. The studio took up the rest of the loft, and it was huge. The studio was filled with paintings and sculpture of an unorthodox nature. A phallic-like protrusion rose from a box, both were covered with canvas and painted in zebra stripes. When the protrusion was lifted and the box held upside down it emitted a mournful, "Maaaa, Maaa. Maaa, Maaa." And there were canvas-covered pyramids painted with psychedelic designs and paintings of geometric shapes and stripes running in different directions. There was one painting of ruby red lips holding a smoldering cigarette.

Mr. Barrows was dressed in a Japanese-style kimono when he answered his door. "What a pleasant surprise," he said, smiling, "come right in." He asked Billy if he would care for wine and cheese and Billy said yes. He hadn't eaten since breakfast that morning. Mr. Barrows poured him a glass of wine and set a piece of cheese before him with a knife and instructions to help himself. Then Mr. Barrows put on an exotic East Indian sitar record. He sat down across from Billy and poured himself a glass of wine. It was deep red burgundy. "Now then, what can I do for you?"

"You can talk to Mr. Hughes and the principal and whoever else ... and ask them not to expel me. I did something awful, Mr. Barrows. I got myself in a lot of trouble, I think."

"Oh, come now. Nothing is as bad as all that. Why don't you tell me about it." Mr. Barrows listened quietly while Billy related the happening in music appreciation.

"I don't understand, Billy," he said when Billy finished, "I mean, for God's sake, *why?* What was the point? I don't get it." Billy shrugged. "I dunno." He looked at Mr. Barrows. No way of understanding, he decided. "I dunno. I just did it." He emptied his wine glass. He got up to leave.

"Do you really feel like that, Billy? Are you so full of hatred for the white and black races that you'd ..."

Billy covered his face with his hand, "Oh, Christ," he said, "I don't know. I don't know. All I knew was they were pushing me, Mr. Barrows, they've *been* pushing me. I had to do something. I had to show them I wasn't a Bernard Leiborwitz."

"I don't think that little speech was a very bright move, Billy. I don't know what *I* can do. Why I'm just hanging in there myself," he laughed. "Me, Peter Barrows, I've got to watch myself around that place. There was a little trouble last year. Talk of firing me. Damn place thinks it has the right to control my personal life!" Billy started walking toward the door. Mr. Barrows went with him.

"Yes, I have to watch my step too, Billy. Here I've studied at the finest schools in New York and Paris, I *almost* was awarded a Guggenheim once ... ah well, and here I am 'watching my step' at Lincoln Junior High School. I'll see what I can do, Billy. I'm not promising anything, but I'll try." He smiled and opened the door. The sitar record was stuck and kept playing the same few notes over and over again.

"Thanks, Mr. Barrows," Billy said and left.

CHAPTER XII

"You'd been warned, Billy," Mr. Hughes said. It was raining outside. It hit the window behind Mr. Hughes desk at a slant. Billy was looking at the rain over the top of Mr. Hughes's head. "Look at me when I'm talking to you," he said. Billy looked at him, fixing his eyes at a point on Mr. Hughes's forehead where the light reflected. "You just don't seem to care, young man. You've made no effort to adjust. Have you? *Have* you? Answer me!" Billy shrugged. "I dunno," he said. He picked at a small paint spot on the knee of his jeans. "No, you haven't, I'm afraid." Mr. Barrows was in Mr. Hughes's office when Billy came. He looked very much the avant-garde painter that morning in his wild print shirt with a scarf tied around his neck and the worn sports jacket with the leather patches sewn on the elbows. Mr. Barrows sat with his thin legs crossed, looking serious and not saying anything while Mr. Hughes talked about Billy's refusing, apparently, to adjust.

"We can't overlook the incident in music appreciation," Mr. Hughes said. "You hurt a lot of kids' feelings in there. You can't go around hurting people's feelings. I won't allow it." He hit his fist mildly on the green blotter covering his desk and it made a dull thud, and he accidently bumped against his desk calendar and knocked it to the floor. He didn't pick it up.

"I've been having a talk with Mr. Barrows here about your paintings. And, we've decided it's more important that a boy learn about his citizenship responsibilities than exhibit some paintings. A good citizen first, a good painter, second."

Billy looked to Mr. Barrows. He wasn't like these other people, was he? Mr. Barrows was still looking serious. He pulled out his pipe and became very occupied with lighting it.

"You will not exhibit any paintings, Billy, not this year."

Mr. Barrows cleared his throat. He was holding the lit pipe in one hand. Blue smoke swirled thinly about his head.

"I agree with Mr. Hughes, Billy. That was quite an uncalled for, uncouth thing you did, you know. You need to be disciplined."

Billy looked out at the gray sky and the rain. He felt empty.

"I'm sorry but you are the one who is at fault. Why, the principal and I were all set to expel you until Mr. Barrows, here ... Well, this is all your own doing, understand?" Mr. Hughes said.

"Okay, that's all. You may be excused.

In art class later, Mr. Barrows took Billy out into the deserted hall and told how it was either the exhibit lost or being expelled. "I'm sorry I couldn't do more." And he went on to talk about how power was always in the hands of the stupid and insensitive and since they were the ones running the show then people like Barrows and Billy would have to learn how to play their game, if only on a superficial level. "And then we're free to do our own thing," he said. Billy thought of the warehouse loft where Mr. Barrows lived and worked and the strange, foolish sculptures and paintings there. Mr. Barrows, free to do his own thing, he though, oh, Mr. Barrows.

Alice Fay had to go talk with Mr. Hughes. She slapped Billy across the face when she got home and told him she'd never been so humiliated in her life and if she had the money she would send him home right then. She said was going down to the BIA office in the morning and see about getting him sent off to an Oklahoma Indian school where they wouldn't coddle him. Then she brought out the sherry and poured herself a glass, and then another, and another until the evening was over.

He lay awake all night, his head feeling as though the pressure was building inside his skull and threatening to crack it and get released.

He didn't get into any more trouble at Lincoln. It wasn't that he had "adjusted" to the situation, as Mr. Hughes had said he should make every effort to do. He didn't want to do any adjusting. He was afraid of adjusting, of losing what he was and becoming someone different, someone tailored to the specifications of Lincoln Junior High School. He got by. Jay El and Haskell, Curtiss and the boys were just as bad as ever but he knew he couldn't fight them any more. He didn't even daydream about beating them up. There were too many of them and this was their place, not his. He ignored their taunts. He put up with their jibes and insults and did nothing, said nothing. Fighting was pointless. He got beat up a few times but after a while they began leaving him alone. He felt more comfortable than before. He was anonymous, unnoticed, almost not there at all.

He thought of going back home to Benewah. But

how would it be? Joe and he sitting around in that little house in the hills, Joe reading his detective magazines and science fiction stories, getting up to walk around from room to room to pace back and forth, looking out the windows at the snow-covered frozen hills. They'd both be restless and dissatisfied and Joe would wish he could go into the town. He'd be anxious for the snow plows to come and clear the roads so he could get to the Big Bear. Billy would have to worry about him again, see him the way he is when he comes home drunk at night. And there was Tom. Tom was there this winter, lying in a cold, lonely grave. Here there was no more to look forward to than on the reservation, no hope, he knew that now. Still, he couldn't go back, not yet.

Alice Fay had gone to see the BIA people about the government school. Billy didn't tell her he wasn't going. She didn't ask him.

"When you go to government school" was something she'd become fond of talking about. When he went to government school, then he'd learn discipline and cleanliness and tidiness and responsibility and things like that. Alice Fay was very caught up in her fantasy of Billy's going away to school. "You'll learn all kinds of wonderful things. They'll take you to the young people's opera rehearsal every year and concerts and I even went to a ballet once. It was lovely. Culture, that's what you'll get, and you'll have work details to attend to each day. That will give you a real sense of responsibility."

He'd separated himself from the denizens of Lincoln and their world. He tried very hard not to notice them.

He remembered a lot, about when he was a little boy, vivid, convivial memories that was almost like having them happen all over again.

127

He went through his days pretending to be going to class and seeing and listening to all that was there, but in his heart he was far, far away.

In his heart he ran over yellow hills and played in deep piny woods and went swimming in the river and rock hunting along the edge. It was just like before, with his mother holding him and touching him with her small, soft hand and singing to him. And there he was standing looking out toward the highway waiting for his big, strong dad to come home from work, a surprise in the glove compartment of the car, or to come home from the hunt, carrying a wide-antlered deer around his neck over his shoulders.

He could see Tom and himself. Tom teaching Billy how to aim a gun, that's it, prop it up, hold it steady against the shoulder, the two boys aiming at tin cans lined on fence posts. Tom and Billy foot racing, Tom slowing down just before the finish, pretending he'd tired out and letting Billy win. And Tom and Billy sitting on the floor on a winter's evening warm by the fire while Waluwetsu told them stories of when the earth was very young and animals talked like people.

His waking hours were full of such memories and he'd become content. It was at night when the trouble came. His dreams were bad.

In his dreams a great whirlwind was in the room where he slept and it would grab him and whirl him around, throwing him up against the walls, and then pluck him up again. He was helpless against the whirlwind's force. He would struggle to free himself, clawing at the walls and trying to get hold of something, anything to stop. It did no good. He knew if he could only reach the door and pass through it then he would be free of the whirlwind and it would be unable to follow. Sometimes he would almost reach the door, he would almost get away, and then he'd be caught again and whirled around and around. He was afraid to sleep and fought against it.

One day a strange thing happened:

Billy was at his locker between classes when suddenly he lost his memory. He had no recollection of any previous existence. He didn't know his name, or how he'd gotten wherever he was. It was as if his life had begun as he was standing there in the hall, as if he'd somehow sprung up full grown from the floor. He looked around and saw all the young Kweauss people rushing, pushing, shoving. He hoped someone would see him, call his name. No one did. The buzzer sounded and there was a clang of locker doors and then the people were suddenly gone and he was left standing all alone in that long, narrow, locker-lined corridor. It was very quiet then, so quiet he could hear his footsteps echo.

He could see this was a school. He was carrying a textbook that said *Your Health* on it and a yellow spiral notebook. He checked both books. In the notebook he found the name: Billy White Hawk and he knew that this was his name.

He wandered through the empty halls until he came to a place marked OFFICE and went inside. The office was empty except for a middle-aged woman in a green dress. She was sitting typing rapidly at a desk.

He didn't say anything. He just stood quietly waiting until she looked up from her work and saw him. She had a narrow, pinched face that looked as if she were suffering mild but annoying pain. She came over to him. He could see the flesh-toned, pink powder thick on the lines in her face.

"Yes, what is it? What can I do for you?" she asked. He was hoping maybe she'd know him. It would feel good to see a person who knew him. She didn't. Her eyes were blank, impatient, glossy. "I, I forgot what my next class is," he told her.

She shook her head disgustedly. "I don't know how anyone could forget what his next class is. It's beyond me ..." She shrugged. "Oh, well, what's your name?"

"Billy White Hawk," he told her. She asked him to spell it and he did. She wrote it down on a slip of paper, silently forming the letters of his name with her pink lips. She opened the file drawer and thumbed through the cards. "Ah, here it is. Algebra II."

"Thank you, ma'am," he said. "Can you tell me the room number, please?" She had lost her place in the card file and was starting to close the drawer. She drew her eyebrows down and together in an expression of annoyance. She looked for it and found it again.

"Room 328," she told him.

"Thanks. Thanks a lot," he said, turning to go. "Third floor, at the top of the stairs," she called after him.

There was an empty desk in room 328 and he sat in it. Little by little, then, it came back to him. His surroundings were familiar again. The school, who he was, where he lived, where he'd come from . . . he remembered it all.

There were two more classes after algebra but Billy didn't stay for them. He wanted to get out of that place, go home where it was safe.

At home he sat on the big chair and stared at the walls. He remembered how awful it had been to be a person with no past, no identity. He wondered what had caused this to happen and if it would happen again. It got dark and he didn't turn on the lights.

He was still sitting there when Alice Fay came home.

"I went to the BIA office again, today," she said. "Oh, it looks good." They'd told her they weren't sure they could take him next fall, they weren't sure there was space, but now it looked like there might be. "I'm just *sure* you'll get in. It's just this feeling I have. How was your day?"

"Okay."

"Good."

The doorbell rang and Alice Fay opened it to Mrs. Mobley. They went into the kitchen and Billy switched on the television set.

Some kids' program was on, a clown and his friends showing cartoons. The clown had a white painted face. He was talking with a hand puppet, a worm named Nathan who used multisyllabled words and wore glasses. Together the clown and Nathan said, "And now boys and girls, get ready cause here's Betty Boop in . . . DOUBLE TROUBLE."

Alice Fay called, "Billy. Billy, come here a sec, will you? Mrs. Mobley has a present for you." He got up and went into the kitchen. More biblical coloring books, he thought. They were drinking coffee and eating cake.

"Hello, Mrs. Mobley," he said. She smiled and nodded. He noticed two strange objects sitting on the kitchen table. She picked one up, gingerly, as if it were very fragile, and handed it to him.

He turned it around in his hand, examining it, wondering what it was supposed to be. It was a plastic bottle of some sort. It had been painstakingly painted in fine swirls of color. He turned it around. He held it and looked to Mrs. Mobley, wondering.

"It's very nice," he told Mrs. Mobley.

She had folded her hands together, pleased that he liked it.

"These little vases (she pronounced it "vahzes"), you know I make them from ordinary plastic containers. Most people use up the shampoo or the dish washing detergent, the underarm deodorant or the nasal mist, and they don't notice the lovely shapes of the bottles. They just throw them away. But not me. I have an eye for beautiful or potentially beautiful things. I take those bottles and I snip off the tops and then paint them. I have many in my place holding paper flowers I've fashioned myself. I believe people should try very hard to surround themselves with beautiful things. Life is so short, we must do the best we can. Too many people go through life not caring, Willy." He winced hearing her call him Willy.

"I think they're cheerful, don't you, Bill?" Alice Fay said.

"Yeah. Thank you very much," he said softly, still holding the bottle gently in his hand and looking at it.

"You're *very* welcome, dear." Mrs. Mobley smiled.

He didn't feel like eating that night. He could only pick at the roast beef TV dinner Alice Fay prepared. His head hurt and he felt profoundly tired.

He lay awake on his davenport bed for hours listening to the sounds of Arnie's Hideaway, the jukebox music and the laughter and the loud talk, all of it blended together and unclear, a rumbling, steady din.

He lay watching the ceiling, thinking of nothing. A cockroach came out of the darkness and hurried across a wide shaft of light, then disappeared again on the other side into the deep shadows.

He felt dizzy the next morning when he tried to stand. All day he lay on the davenport. His head hurt. He felt tired. When Alice Fay came home she took his temperature and found he had a fever. By that night he'd become very sick and fell into delirium. He was not aware of being moved but of being in another room. It was a white room with smooth walls and above was a white ceiling. He looked up at the acoustical tiles on the ceiling and they seemed far, far away. It was like he was lying on the very bottom of something looking up at the surface he could not reach.

The delirium kept his mind in a warm, pleasant fog. He was aware of Alice Fay, the doctors and nurses. I'm dying, he thought, and he was not afraid. He didn't know it would be so easy. He remembered a serial in the Sunday paper he was following. He told them to bring it, that he had to see it. He'd been following this adventure for five weeks and he had to know how it turned out.

He saw himself down by the river in Benewah searching for rocks. It was not possible to distinguish his imaginings from reality. He was enjoying himself looking for rocks.

Then he saw himself lying in a birch canoe floating along down the river. His eyes were closed and his hands were folded over his chest. The sun was warm on his face. He was lying very still.

Alongside the river were dense trees and people talked and moved about in the shadows of the trees. He could not tell what these people were saying. There was a soft roaring sound, like continuous thunder. The roaring was becoming louder. The canoe traveled swiftly along the narrow, twisting river.

He heard a strange sound, a low, chantlike sound and he recognized what it was; the owl's song.

The owl's song. And he understood then what the people by the river's edge were saying. "The waterfalls," they were saying, "the waterfalls."

They were warning him, look out for the falls. He was heading for the falls. He tried to move, to open his eyes. He could only lie still, lying in the canoe with his hands folded over his heart. He heard someone scream and knew it was himself.

"No, no, I don't want to die. I don't want to die!" he shouted.

But the owl's song . . . Manitous telling of a coming death, speaking with the owl's voice. Manitous don't change their minds or make mistakes! Oh, but he didn't want to die!

He reached out his hand and felt that someone had taken it, a strong, sure hand, rough and calloused. He hung on until the river and canoe and owl's song had gone away. He awoke and a young nurse asked him how he felt and took his pulse and temperature and said he was doing fine. He asked her where his father was, that he'd like to see him. But his father wasn't there. He'd not *been* there, either, but she'd call his sister if he wanted, she said.

Joe. He had been there, though, in some way. He remembered he'd heard the owl's song and it hadn't been for himself, after all. Joe. He'd have to go see Joe. He fell into a deep, restful, natural sleep.

CHAPTER XIII

The rain had been coming down most every day and every night for a long time; so long it began to seem like this was the ordinary—the way all days were and other times were hard to recall.

Then the rain stopped. The clouds thinned and parted and in the early afternoon Billy was awakened by the sun shining in his face. He got up and pushed the window open and let the cold, rain-cleared air inside. It was windy outside: he could see the wind blowing scraps of paper down the street, and the hair and clothing of passers-by. He was aware of being hungry, very, very hungry and he went into the kitchen and scrambled himself six eggs and ate them quickly. Afterward he left the frying pan unwashed on top of the stove and the dishes he used lying in the sink.

It had been some time; four weeks or more since he'd been outside, since the awful sickness. He was weak and listless for a long time but now he was better and he was tired of being cooped up in Alice Fay's pristine little apartment.

He dressed and went outside. Two of the men who slept in the doorways and on the street around there were sitting out in front of the apartment building near the mailboxes. They smiled at Billy and told him good morning. They had a gallon of red wine with a newly broken seal and they asked him if he'd like to join them in a drink.

"If you're in no hurry. Maybe you got somewhere more important?" one of them said. He squatted down near the two men. They handed him the jug and he took a small swig. It was cheap, bad-tasting stuff. "Nice weather," he said.

"Eh? What's that?"

Billy pointed up to the sky. There was a place where you could see a patch of blue, and it seemed to be clearing more.

"I say, nice weather. Rain's gone."

"Ah." The men nodded and laughed, "Thank the

135

Lord. So wet it was a man couldn't get any sleep."

"Sherman here and me, why we had to get *hotel rooms*," the other said.

"Hotel rooms?" Billy repeated, incredulous. How could *they* rent hotel rooms.

"Yeah. The Salvation Army was all filled up. Here you wanna another shot?"

"Ah, no thanks." The man had just taken a long shot before offering the bottle to Billy. Now he shrugged, then took another drink, the rose-colored liquid bubbling in the neck of the bottle.

"Here, Sherm." Sherm took the jug.

"We even staged a fight but nobody took notice of us. No cops hauled us in. Damn po-lice anyway. Can't find one when you need one! We *had* to get rooms. It cut into our grocery money but a man can't sleep in the rain, can he?"

"No, sir, he sure can't." He wondered how they could afford it.

"Say, do you mind if I ask where you got the money," he asked.

"Where we always get money, naturally," the one called Sherman answered.

"The P.B."

"The P.B.? What's that?" Billy asked.

"The *P.B.* You know . . . the *Plasma Bank*."

"What's that? What do you do to get money there?" .

The two men looked at each other. Sherman shook his head as if to say how could anybody be so dumb.

"We sell our plasma. Ten bucks a pint. We lay there on a table and they take blood out of our arms. Then they take the plasma out of the blood and put the blood, minus plasma, back in again. Simple, no? Savvy?" The two men laughed amusedly.

"Say, that sounds good," Billy said. "Could I do that too?"

"Sure, just so long as you're eighteen. You are, aren't ya?"

"Yeah. Say, could you tell me how to get there?"

The men gave him directions how to get to the Plasma Bank. It was only a few blocks away. He went and they believed his lie about his age ... He sold his plasma and they gave him ten dollars in two new, crisp fives. Enough for a bus ticket home, and that was what he was going to spend it on. He felt good about going, anxious to get there and see Joe. He didn't know what he would do there. All he knew was for now he had to get back. Worry about the rest later. He folded the fives and put them in his shirt pocket and went back to the apartment.

"Dear Alice Fay," he wrote, "thanks for everything. Someday I'll pay you back. Love, Billy." He reread the note, then scribbled out the word "Love" and wrote "Sincerely" above it. He put the note on Alice Fay's smoothly made bed.

He packed his things in the army duffel bag, slung it over his shoulder. He started out the door, then, remembering the two men on the sidewalk, came back and took a fifth of Alice Fay's sipping sherry from the cupboard.

"Bless you, my boy," one of the men said when he gave them the bottle. They'd already finished the first jug they'd had earlier.

CHAPTER XIV

It was springtime now and the last snow had fallen a month ago but the snow remained covering the Benewah hills, dry and frozen, blue-white in the early morning. The truck driver Billy'd hitched a ride with was lonely and he'd been driving a long time. He had a long ways yet to go. He tried to make friendly conversation but it was hard for Billy to respond.

"You from here, young fella? Where you comin' from?" he asked, and Billy answered him. He said his father wasn't well and he'd had to come home. He wondered if Joe would be there. It had been so long and they'd not kept in touch. What if something happened? He remembered how he'd heard the owl's song the night he was sick and afraid. If Joe died would Etta and Nicademus, would anybody, let him know?

He saw the old place and it felt good seeing it again, so small and white there before the big, dark wooded hills. And Joe was there, all right. The pickup truck was sitting in the yard in front of the house. But something was strange . . . there was no smoke coming up out of the chimney. Joe should've started a fire by now, or even kept one going all night.

"This next road, here, mister. That's our place over there." The driver nodded. He stopped in front of the mailbox and Billy jumped down.

"Thanks a lot," he told the driver, "have a good trip."

"Hope everything turns out okay for your old man," the driver said. Billy started hurriedly down the road toward home.

The road had been muddy, probably yesterday, and the tire tracks were deep ruts, frozen hard now, with high ridges between and there was a place where there'd been trouble, where the tires had spun and dug deeper and deeper, splattering mud far on the white snow and another set of tires, big wide ones, had come and helped free them from the mud. The thin, frozen ridges the tire marks made in the dirt broke and crumbled under Billy's boots as he walked.

He found his father trying to get a fire going in the old wood burner. He smiled. He gripped Billy's hand hard and slapped him heavily on the back. His hair in those months Billy was gone had become nearly all white now. Joe laughed. "Well, well, well. So you're back, are you?" And slapped Billy on the back again.

"Take it easy, Dad," Billy laughed, "you're going to knock the wind out of me."

"Look here, son. I forgot to get kindling wood in last night. Went out this morning and got some. Too wet. Just too wet. No use, look here." He showed him the kindling wood he'd been trying to work with. He was right, it was too wet to burn. "It'll be okay soon, Dad," Billy told him, "we can use newspaper to get the fire going now. You got newspapers?" Joe shook his head no. "Then how about magazines?" They used some of his old detective magazines and built a fire. By noon the awful chill was gone and the little house was warm.

Billy wanted to talk deeply with him. He wanted to tell his father how he'd gone to that place, that

139

city, and saw these things, and known these people and come back knowing it was not right for him, *out there*, that he'd come back hoping to find it better at home. It had never been easy talking to Joe.

"How've you been, Dad," he asked, "all this time? I worried about you."

"Oh, you know me. I look out for myself. I get by." Joe laughed. "I was sort of sick for awhile but it's all over with now. Strong as a bull again." He hit his stomach with his fist. "And you? Tell me, how was it? Are you going back?" Billy shook his head. "I don't think so. I don't know what I'm going to do, Dad. Not go back to that place for sure. Stay around here for a while. Maybe for a long while, Dad."

"I see. You know I'm happy to have you back."

"Tell me, Dad, about your manhood vision? Tell me about how you became Sah-húlt-sum."

His father smiled a faint, little smile and looked far away with his one good eye. At last he said, "I can't. To tell the truth, I don't remember too well. Anyway, all that was a long, long time ago."

Then for long minutes they sat together in silence. Strange, Billy thought, how he'd forgotten how *completely* quiet it was here . . . no knocking of pipes, no humming of refrigerator . . . nothing.

The sun came out bright and strong and melted the snow away. The waters of the river ran high and swift and made roaring noise. A month passed. And then another. It was almost summer now.

Billy learned from Etta how strange Joe was while he was gone.

"He forgets things, Bill. He forgets when he's supposed to go to work and he forgets to cut wood. He forgets to eat and I've come over here at noontime and found him still lying in bed. 'No reason to get up,' he said. And a couple of times he was talking about you like you were still around. I tried talking to him. I said, 'Joe, come live with us, Joe. We got lot of room in our new house. You shouldn't be living alone. You're too old, now, Joe,' but he wouldn't do it. Stubborn, that man, just plain stubborn is all."

But since he'd come home Billy didn't notice any of this strangeness. At times he was a little forgetful, it was true, but at times so was he and so was everyone, weren't they? It was nothing. Joe was fine. So was he. He felt fine. He didn't worry about what was going to happen any more, he just lived each day as well as he could and it seemed good. There was a new calmness, somehow, come over him.

One morning Joe told Billy to go into town and get some groceries and have the spare tire fixed. (He'd been letting Billy drive the pickup but this would be the first time he'd do it all alone.) Joe was sitting out on the front steps when Billy left, wearing his reading glasses and filing his saws. He could hear the grating, metallic sound of the file scraping between the points of the saw from a long way away.

He bought the groceries, then walked around the town, looking in store windows, taking his time. It was warm and sunshiny, a very pleasant sort of morning for walking around and taking in the town.

It was noon when he got back. Joe was not there. He looked around for him and found him in the woods out back. He'd chopped down a tree, a big, thick-trunked tree. He had his shirt off and he was sweating. He was chopping the tree up into logs now. His face was red and flushed. He smiled when he saw Billy. He spoke happily, short of breath, "Just like the old days. Just like it used to

141

be." He swung the ax high over his head and brought it down, splitting a log.

"Dad!" Billy shouted, "Dad, you know, you shouldn't." Joe swung the ax again, brought it down, let it rest, caught in the wood. He stood up straight. He wiped the sweat from his brow. He laughed, full and strong, and his laugh sounded thunderously loud in the quiet woods. He laughed again. "Yes, yes I should. Now, go away, boy. Go away. I got work to do." And began chopping again.

Billy knew he couldn't make him stop. He went back to the woodshed and got the other ax. He could help, though, he could take some of that work himself.

All day long they worked together chopping logs. Billy would become tired and want to rest, then look at Joe. Joe wouldn't slow down. He kept on and on, seemingly tireless. Strong he was, as he said, strong as a bull, and not old . . . no, not old at all. Joe grinned at Billy, a happy strong grin and Billy felt that he'd caught a glimpse of Joe as he was once, Joe just-like-in-the-old-days. Billy grinned at Joe and they went on working. By nightfall the exhilaration was gone for both, and they were tired but the job was finished.

Joe didn't feel like eating, he said, his voice weak and hoarse as if he'd had a bad cold. He wanted to lie down on his bed and rest awhile.

Joe died that evening. He died peacefully in his sleep. A heart attack the doctor said when he came. A man his age, and he shook his head, an old man like Joe should've known to take it easy. Splitting logs, he should've known better.

It was all right, though. Billy knew it was good that it happened this way, with his last day being one spent in hard work like "the old days." It was all right.

CHAPTER XV

It was a good day near the end of the summer after the spring Sah-húlt-sum died that the vision came to him (or the vision came to him long before he recognized it as such).

He was looking out over the hills where crops of grain grew ripe and tall, shimmering under the sun, and a breeze passed through the fields making ripples. He remembered the ocean he'd watched back there when he was with Alice Fay. He remembered the day he'd gone down by the edge of the sea and stared long out over the water and how he'd seen a strange thing: an oceangoing fishing canoe way out in the mist, the white foam raised with the rise and fall of the rowers' paddles. He remembered how he'd quickly dismissed it as an optical illusion.

It was his vision, he knew now. He remembered Sah-húlt-sum, the warrior, the son of White Hawk and how sad he'd felt that Sah-húlt-sum was at first unsure of his manhood vision, and later had forgotten it.

Billy White Hawk was his man's name. He needed no other. He looked up into the blue summer skies where soft, billowy white clouds drifted. He saw a bird soaring there, its black feathers glistening in the sunlight. Soon now, the summer would be over, he thought, then he'd have to make plans. He'd have to go away but not back *there* again. He'd go away and it would be different, yet, he knew it would be all right. He was Billy White Hawk, he'd been sent his vision. He was a man like Sah-húlt-sum had been, like White Hawk had been and he would always be.

He loved these Benewah hills, this place where the people of his tribe first came into being when the earth was very young. It was, as Waluwetsu had said, that there was very little of what had been. It seemed there was no way of staying and living any more. Still, all this would remain with him when he went away and would not change. He was the son of Sah-húlt-sum, the grandson of White Hawk, the tribe's last shaman.

He heard singing begin and he looked all around him and could see no one. The singing became stronger and he realized it came from deep within his being.

> Wa-ya-neh
> Wa-ya-neh
> Wa-ya-neh, ya-na

Clear and strong his song rang out that day near the end of the Benewah summer.

> Wa-ya-neh,
> Wa-ya-neh,
> Wa-ya-neh, ya-na

It was all right, now. It was all right. Manitous, spirits of earth, wind, rain, sun. Father and grandfather and unknown ancestors. Benewah country and Lapwai and Clearwater, oceans, deserts, cities, it was all the same, now. It was all right.